The moment their lips met, a rush of sensation shuddered through Elizabeth's veins

She eased closer to him, her hands sliding down the smooth leather of his jacket, then struggling to reach the bare flesh beneath.

She'd never experienced a touch like Seth's. He had only to look at her to awaken her passion. She'd missed him. Dear heaven, how she'd missed him.

Her hands hesitantly slipped beneath the edge of his jacket. But as her cold fingertips clutched the fabric of his shirt, he drew back.

"We've got to stop. We can't do this," he whispered. "Not here. Not like this."

Then when? Seth's rejection hurt more than she ever would have thought possible.

"Don't read my words the wrong way, Lizzie," he whispered. "I want you. I want you more than life itself at this moment." He shook his head as if to clear it of the lingering wisps of abandonment. "But I won't make love to you when a killer might be waiting and watching."

The reminder hit her like a cool douse of water.

They were still in danger.

Incredible danger…

ABOUT THE AUTHOR

Lisa Bingham is a resident of Tremonton, Utah—a rural farming community where the sounds of birds and the rustle of wheat can still be heard on hot summer evenings. She has written both historical and contemporary romances and loves spending time watching her characters grow. When she isn't writing, she spends time with her husband on his three-hundred-acre farm and teaches English at a local middle school.

Books by Lisa Bingham

HARLEQUIN INTRIGUE
540—WHEN THE NIGHT DRAWS NEAR

HARLEQUIN AMERICAN ROMANCE
602—NANNY JAKE
635—THE BUTLER AND THE BACHELORETTE
651—THE DADDY HUNT
662—DANA AND THE CALENDAR MAN
692—THE PRINCESS AND THE FROG

Don't miss any of our special offers. Write to us at the following address for information on our newest releases.

Harlequin Reader Service
U.S.: 3010 Walden Ave., P.O. Box 1325, Buffalo, NY 14269
Canadian: P.O. Box 609, Fort Erie, Ont. L2A 5X3

When Night Draws Near
Lisa Bingham

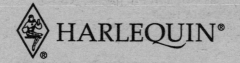

HARLEQUIN®

TORONTO • NEW YORK • LONDON
AMSTERDAM • PARIS • SYDNEY • HAMBURG
STOCKHOLM • ATHENS • TOKYO • MILAN • MADRID
PRAGUE • WARSAW • BUDAPEST • AUCKLAND

To Dad, his Cessna and fond memories of flying.
Thanks to you, I've never been afraid.

ISBN 0-373-22540-7

WHEN NIGHT DRAWS NEAR

Copyright © 1999 by Lisa Bingham

This edition published by arrangement with Harlequin Books S.A.

® and TM are trademarks of the publisher. Trademarks indicated with ® are registered in the United States Patent and Trademark Office, the Canadian Trade Marks Office and in other countries.

Visit us at www.romance.net

Printed in U.S.A.

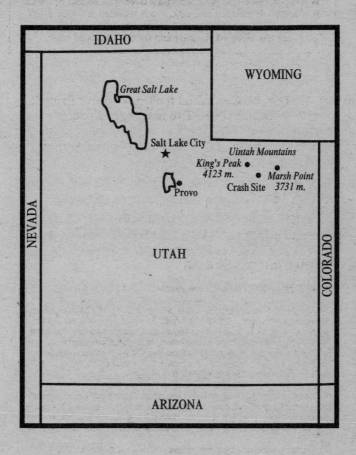

CAST OF CHARACTERS

Elizabeth Boothe—Terrified of flying, she never thought that a much-dreaded shuttle to Denver would force her to confront her fear of planes—as well as the one man she has never forgotten.

Seth Brody—A routine charter flight to Denver offers him the unexpected opportunity of confronting his ex-wife and the mistakes of his past.

Frankie Webb—A convicted serial killer with nothing to lose, he's willing to do anything to escape.

Stan Kowalski and Brent Caldwell—They've both invested a lifetime in their careers with the FBI, and they're not about to let a prisoner escape on their watch.

Willa Hawkes—A lonely librarian, she's delivering a stack of rare original documents to an upcoming exhibit.

Michael Nealy—Scientist and social misfit, he's on his way to Aruba and the start of happier times.

Peter Walsh—With his bank about to be audited and his life in turmoil, he merely wants a little more time to sort out his personal affairs.

Ernst Gallegher—A powerful corporate executive, he has little time or patience for anything but his own agenda.

Richard Brummel—"Sticky Ricky" has managed to steal one of the greatest chocolate-chip-cookie recipes of all time...if he can only manage to survive long enough to enjoy it.

Prologue

"Mayday, mayday, mayday!"

The words pricked Elizabeth Boothe's consciousness, bursting the warm bubble of sleep and yanking her abruptly into the real world.

Something was horribly wrong.

Even as a part of her begged to return to the blissful ignorance of her dreams, Elizabeth's eyes blinked and she fought to focus. Hazily, she tried to fathom what had awakened her from a particularly heavy sleep.

"Mayday, mayday, mayday!"

The full meaning of the distress call being issued by the pilot had barely registered before Elizabeth was thrown against the restraint of her seat belt. A cry burst from her lips and she automatically braced her hands against the chilling glass of the windshield. Bit by bit, she absorbed her surroundings, even as her brain continued to function much more sluggishly.

A plane. She was on a plane.

And the plane was going down.

Panic rose in Elizabeth's throat, choking her. Why had she fallen asleep? If she'd been awake, she could have...

She could have done what? She wasn't a pilot. She didn't even like flying.

From behind her, someone shouted, "Dear God, we're out of control!"

Glancing over her shoulder, Elizabeth registered the owner of the voice, an older woman with short-cropped iron-gray hair. The woman's features were a study in panic as she grappled with her seat belt.

Elizabeth knew that woman. She'd talked to her. Hadn't she?

In a seat nearby, a baby-faced boy-man hugged his rucksack. Piercing gray-green eyes stared wide from a face that had grown ashen—a face that had probably never known real fear. Across the aisle, another man lunged for an airsick bag, and in doing so, he offered a glimpse of the pistol holstered beneath his arm.

Older woman. Boy-man. FBI agent.

The identifiers scrambled in her brain refusing to make sense. Somehow, she knew these people. But she'd taken something that had made her sleepy and dull-witted. A pill...*pills.*

Why couldn't she think?

The plane bucked again, and the violent sawing motion forced her to wedge one hand more tightly against the window and the other against the arm of her seat.

Shaking her head to clear it, she tried to ignore the scene around her. Surely, this was all a dream. A nightmare...

"Mayday, damn it!"

The expletive caused her to glance at the pilot. Suddenly every incident leading up to this moment was excruciatingly clear.

Seth Brody was her pilot.

Seth Brody.

The man she'd married after knowing him less than a week. The man she'd left after less than a month. The man she'd avoided for more than three years.

Seth was flying the plane.

And it was about to crash.

Chapter One

"Listen, Paul," Elizabeth Boothe said into her cellular phone, interrupting her employer's harangue. "It's not my fault that Greg Russell didn't show up for our appointment today. He was delayed in Toronto. He called from Canada early this morning, offered his profuse apologies, and stated he would have to reschedule the meeting for some time next week."

Paul Burbank sighed. "Damn it, Elizabeth. I told you to send one of your underlings to talk to Russell. I needed you here at the main offices, not in some godforsaken corner of Idaho."

"Utah," she corrected.

"Same thing. I wanted you here to help with the finishing touches on the Allied Foods account. How could you have overlooked my implicit instructions?"

Elizabeth grimaced. "We've been through all this

before, Paul. Greg Russell is offering us a multi-million dollar account.''

''*If* you can ever pin the man down long enough for conferencing.''

''Which is why I came to Utah.''

''But Allied Foods—''

Elizabeth sighed, reaching for the huge leather satchel she used as a combined briefcase and carry-on bag.

Originally, the Allied Foods presentation had been scheduled for next week, but when rumors of the competitor's plans had surfaced, Paul had bumped up the date.

So why was it suddenly her fault that she wasn't in New York to pitch the ideas? Supposedly, Paul was in charge of the project. Despite the fact that she'd left him with detailed notes, layouts and graphics, he wanted her glued at his side so that she could answer all the questions he couldn't.

Before he claimed her idea as his own.

''Paul,'' she said wearily. ''I'm doing everything I can to be in New York by noon tomorrow.''

Everything including booking myself on a charter jet.

She absently wiped her palms against the heavy wool of her coat. Years ago, she'd sworn she would never succumb to charter services. Elizabeth was the first to admit that she was a white-knuckle traveler who preferred large planes, first-class accommodations, a double dose of motion-sickness medication and a stiff drink. In that order.

She didn't like to fly.

She'd never liked flying.

Even though her ex-husband—a Ph.D. in the fields of history and warfare aviation—had been a pilot who augmented his salary as a professor at NYU by performing with national air shows. He flew restored "toy" planes and shot restored "toy" guns to amuse slack-jawed audiences too caught up in the excitement to realize that every time the pilots took to the air, they put their lives on the line.

Her stomach knotted at the memory—as well as the sickening dread she felt each time she approached an airport. Elizabeth switched the cell phone to her opposite ear. Absently, she began pulling her day planner, cosmetic bag, reading glasses and magazines out of her bag. All the while, she searched for the tiny brass pillbox that contained her airsickness medicine.

"Aha!" she breathed when she found the container beneath the latest issue of the *Wall Street Journal*.

"Did you say something?" Paul asked irritably.

"No. Go ahead."

Truth be told, she couldn't remember what Paul had been complaining about last—and she didn't bother to listen when he did resume speaking. She shook three pills into her palm and downed them with a gulp of the bottled water she always carried when she traveled. Then, considering the itty-bitty plane she was about to board—in contrast to a 747— she swallowed two more. All the while, Paul Burbank, the CEO of Radon Advertising, droned in her ear like an irritating wasp.

Come on, come on, Elizabeth silently urged the driver of the cab. When Greg Russell had called from Canada to explain his delay, Elizabeth had immediately called the hotel travel agent in the hopes of returning to New York earlier than planned. But bad weather in the midwestern states and an emergency landing on one of the major runways at Salt Lake International Airport had delayed or canceled dozens of flights. Elizabeth's only chance of leaving the area before morning was to catch a commuter flight from the Million-Air Municipal Airport on the outskirts of Salt Lake City. From there, she could journey to Denver where she would be able to transfer to a commercial airline bound for New York City.

Unfortunately, the commuter flight was scheduled to leave at four twenty-five.

Elizabeth squinted at her watch. Four-fifteen. Hadn't it been four-fifteen when she left the hotel?

Panicked, she regarded the shadows creeping into the cab, wondering if her watch was playing tricks on her. Had she forgotten to wind it? Had she already missed her flight?

Frowning, she tapped the crystal and lifted it to her ear. But the steady ticking of her mother's old timepiece assured her that the hour it showed was correct. Despite the darkness already gathering around the snow-swept countryside, evening was still hours away.

Elizabeth bent and peered out the slush-spattered window into the gloom of the afternoon. Silently, she prayed that the Midwest's blizzards weren't contagious. If the weather got much worse, air traffic would be brought to a standstill.

She shivered as she noted the heavy clouds piled against the stark mountain range. Wisps of vapor spilled over the valley ceiling like phantom fingers, muting the colors of the afternoon.

Ashes. It was as if the countryside were dusted with ashes.

Granted, the eerie darkness wasn't due entirely to the oppressive clouds. Here in the mountains, nighttime came early. When the eerie twilight was combined with the ever-present inversion caused by something the locals called "the lake effect" the result could be especially claustrophobic.

Especially to someone about to fly out of this place in a plane no bigger than a vintage Buick.

"Couldn't Russell have told you two days ago that he wouldn't be able to meet you as planned?" Paul insisted.

Since Paul had offered a direct question, Elizabeth had no choice but to respond.

"I don't think Russell knew anything until he was notified that his latest shipment hadn't cleared customs."

To Elizabeth's relief, the lights of the municipal airport winked at her out of the gloom.

"Listen, Paul, I've got to go," she said quickly, grasping at any excuse to terminate the call. "I've only got five minutes to make my plane."

"But, Elizabeth, I—"

"I'll talk to you tomorrow," she said firmly, punching the end button and tossing the phone into her voluminous bag. It was quickly followed by the rest of the gear she'd scattered over the back seat of the taxicab.

Checking the meter bolted to the cab's dashboard, she handed the driver a fifty as he rolled to a stop in front of a clapboard building that announced itself as the Home of Western Skies Charter.

The hiss of the tires against the slush in the gutter had barely subsided when she threw open her door and ran to the terminal, juggling her carry-on, her leather portfolio case and suit bag.

"Hey, lady!" the driver called as he rolled down the curbside window. "Your fare was only thirteen bucks!"

"Keep the change," she shouted as she rushed through the automatic sliding door.

Only one counter displayed the Western Skies logo, so Elizabeth bolted in that direction, her stomach knotting when she noted the call letters for her flight scribbled on a white board, but no attendant.

Had she missed it? Had her flight left?

Panting from her efforts to carry her things and navigate the slippery tile floor in high heels, Elizabeth caught sight of a shape bent behind the counter and offered a silent prayer of gratitude.

"Please…can you…tell me if the flight…to…"

The words escaped between quick gasps for air. Then, before she could inhale and push away the faintness caused by a week of intermittent meals, too many flights, nerve-racking delays and a heavy dose of motion-sickness pills, the man turned. Stared.

Elizabeth felt her body change into a block of ice as she gazed into that all-too-familiar face.

"You," she whispered hoarsely.

Then she stood rooted in space and time as—for one tense minute of silence—the tall, lean figure stared at her as if he too had seen a mirage. Life around her skidded into slow motion.

Seth Brody.

Her ex-husband.

She watched with something akin to horror as Seth straightened, towering over her. His eyes narrowed and his lips thinned into a straight, uncompromising line. Then he set down the clipboard he held and circled the counter.

With each step he took, her pulse throbbed, her heart clenched.

It had been so long since she'd been near him; she'd convinced herself that she would never see him again. But in a freak encounter, she was forced to confront the one man that she'd so carefully avoided for years.

"Elizabeth?"

Her name was little more than a whisper, but Seth managed to communicate much more than a mere greeting. Buried in the syllables were the seeds of shock, recrimination, disbelief and regret.

Elizabeth squeezed her eyes shut and prayed for calm. Never in her wildest dreams had she thought that she would meet Seth here. Like this.

Maybe I shouldn't have taken five pills.

Generally, Elizabeth's body was resistant to all sorts of medication, so she tended to take an extra aspirin or an extra cough lozenge. But there was a limit to any person's tolerance—even hers. Surely, this hallucination was nothing more than the result of the over-the-counter motion-sickness drugs.

But when she dared to look again, it was to discover that Seth was very real. He'd moved closer, crowding her, shutting off her supply of air.

"Elizabeth?" he breathed.

Without warning, his hands slid into her hair, tangling into the tight knot at the back of her head, and drawing her up to meet his savage kiss.

Her eyes closed as pleasure swamped her. The white-hot passion, the instantaneous desire. Seth had always inspired such a reaction. In the past, he had only to look at her to make her weak. And when he touched her...

She became his slave.

A moan seeped from her throat. Her hands slid over his chest and she gripped the worn leather of his vintage bomber jacket. Although her knees trembled, she struggled to anchor herself in reality as the world whirled out of sight and left her stranded on an island of sensation.

As much as she hated to admit it, Seth felt so good—and he made *her* feel good. So alive, so vital, so feminine.

Heedless of the consequences, Elizabeth strained closer, and closer, pressing herself to hard planes and angles that her body hungered to experience once again. Just once.

When he broke away, gasping for breath, she offered an unconscious sob, then covered her aching lips with her fingertips. Hesitantly, she stared up at him, watching his expression shift from one of hunger…to one of denial—

To a hard acceptance of the realities of the past.

This man had once been her husband. But it was Elizabeth who'd left. Elizabeth who'd given up on the relationship.

She wrenched away from him, knowing that if she allowed him to hold her again, even for a few scant minutes, she would forget everything that had driven her from Seth Brody's side. She would forget everything she'd accomplished in the past few years, the courage she'd gained and the successes she'd won.

Sinking to her knees, she began to gather the items that had spilled from her bags. She didn't remember dropping them. She didn't remember much of anything at all other than the way her body had tensed in excitement at seeing Seth for the first time in three years.

Her fingers shook, making the simple task inordinately difficult. She had the sudden sensation of topping the rise to an enormous runaway roller coaster. Events, emotions, sensations had launched her life out of control, and she had no idea when she could expect her equilibrium to return.

"Ladies and gentlemen. Western Skies, Flight 365 for Denver has been delayed for twenty minutes so that plows can clear the runway," a voice announced from a nearby exit. "Feel free to take your seats in the plane if you'd like, or you may relax here in the terminal. We'll begin formal boarding at four thirty-five."

Elizabeth glanced briefly at the plump, middle-aged woman who stood near a metal fire door leading outside. Lifting a hand, the woman motioned for those passengers who wished to board the plane to accompany her.

She had to go.

Escape.

But as much as she longed to run, Elizabeth couldn't move. For long seconds, she stared at the tips of Seth's scuffed work boots.

A broad, masculine hand stretched into view, and before she could react, Seth took her elbow, lifting Elizabeth to her feet.

Her brain ordered her to stand, toss him a careless farewell and hustle onto her plane. Instead, she swallowed hard, attempting to dislodge the knot of tension that had formed in her throat. "Th-that's my flight," she whispered.

"They've been delayed."

"Yes, but—"

"Relax. They won't leave without you."

"But—"

"*I'm* waiting for clearance from the ground crew as well as three more passengers. I can't leave until they show up."

Elizabeth stared up at him as the full import of his statement sunk into her head.

"*You're* the pilot?"

"Yes."

Damn, damn, damn. Why hadn't she thought of such a possibility when she'd bought her ticket?

But then, she hadn't known that Seth was flying

with a charter company. The last time she'd seen him, he'd still been with the air shows and the National Arts and Humanities Endowment. How was she to have guessed that he'd transferred his allegiance to the private sector?

Distantly, Elizabeth knew that Seth was waiting for her to say something. The air had locked in her lungs. Her muscles were gripped in icy disbelief.

A part of her cataloged everything about him—his longish, ash-brown hair, sparkling gray-green eyes, rough-hewn features. Another part of her clung to the startling fact that Seth Brody was the pilot of this particular flight.

"I—I don't understand," she finally murmured, since he was waiting for a response and she didn't know what else to say.

"What's to understand? I'm the person flying you to Denver." When Elizabeth didn't comment, he added, "I own Western Skies."

Her knees threatened to buckle. Afraid she would embarrass herself by falling on the floor at his feet, she abandoned her baggage altogether. Moving on wooden legs, she sank into one of the nearby vinyl chairs provided for waiting passengers.

"I didn't know that you'd abandoned the...the air shows."

Seth planted his hands on his hips, making her that much more aware of the whipcord leanness of his body, the flinty cast to his features. He looked older, tougher and more resolute than ever.

"My work with the air shows was due to a temporary grant project from the National Arts and Humanities Endowment. You knew that.''

She frowned, trying to remember. But all she could fathom was that her ex-husband was standing only a few feet away—and that event was far more unsettling than she would have believed possible.

The leaden knot of apprehension that had formed in her stomach the moment she'd booked a charter flight increased, battling with the medication she'd taken. A clammy sweat broke out on her forehead. Her fingertips tingled as if chilled.

She should have trusted her instincts. She should have known that there was a reason she'd dreaded the upcoming flight. Some innate sixth sense must have known that...

That what? That she would see Seth again?

Or that she would not feel completely vindicated when she did so?

Go. Get out of here. Forget you ever meant to take this flight before it's too late.

Elizabeth breathed deeply. "Seth, I—"

Before she could finish, the main door opened in a flurry of wind and slush. Elizabeth bit her lip as her eyes dodged from two dark blue–suited figures in trench coats to the orange-clad, chain-shackled prisoner they led between them.

The men were making a beeline for Elizabeth, and seeing their arrival as a perfect distraction for a clean getaway, she jumped to her feet. Without pausing to think of the consequences of her actions, she darted to the spot where her luggage was still heaped on the floor. Slinging the straps over her shoulders, she prepared to leave, but found her way blocked by the trio. The two men in suits held out their identification for Seth to study. From a point behind him, even Elizabeth could see the FBI insignias.

"Sorry to keep you waiting," the older, grizzled agent said as he slid the documents into his trench coat. "I'm Stan Kowalski, and this is my partner Brent Caldwell. We had some trouble with traffic."

Seth shot Elizabeth a "we'll talk later" look before offering aloud, "No problem. We're waiting for the runways to be cleared, so we've got a few minutes."

Seth's response was calm and professional, and Elizabeth wondered if he were used to this sort of thing—ferrying the FBI and their prisoners to Denver.

She, on the other hand, had taken one look at the convict and her heart had leapt into her throat. She wasn't so involved in her career that she didn't recognize the man's features and slim build. Frankie Webb. An alleged serial killer who had already been convicted of two murders. If the news accounts were to be believed, he'd killed at least eleven women, all of them in their early thirties. Women who were slender, with dark hair, dark eyes and a medium build.

Just like me.

Webb's eyes caught her scrutiny. Elizabeth shuddered when his lips twitched in the barest of smiles.

"Where should we stow our luggage?" Stan asked, indicating the two small canvas bags being held by his partner.

"Patty, can you get Billy to come retrieve these bags?"

The woman at the door waved, and within seconds, a young kid dressed in the Western Skies uniform loped forward to meet them.

Seth moved to retrieve two identification tags for the agents, and as he did, Frankie leaned toward her, his brown-black eyes glinting.

"Do you know what I like about little girls like you?"

Gooseflesh prickled on Elizabeth's arms. She wanted to run—or at least step back—but she stood rooted to the spot.

Stan Kowalski jerked on Frankie's arm, tugging him away. "Behave yourself, Frankie." The agent nodded in Elizabeth's direction. "Sorry, ma'am. We've got a prisoner with no manners, but we'll keep him in line."

Frankie offered an insolent grin, then tugged on his cuffs, rattling the chains in a way that was meant to disconcert her.

Stan glared at him, but it was the FBI agent who won the momentary battle of wills. Evidently deciding that it wasn't worth the effort of needling the men, Frankie tried a different tack.

"I'd like to get a drink before we board."

"This isn't a pleasure cruise, Billy," Stan said stiffly.

"Water. I'm talkin' about a drink of water. From the fountain." When the men ignored him, Frankie shouted, "I demand to see my lawyer! Denyin' a guy of a drink of water is against his civil rights. I'll have the ACLU climbin' all over you.''

Without pause, Stan slammed his charge against a concrete support post, whipped an under cover nightstick from his pocket, and leveled his *coup baton* against Frankie's throat. "Listen up, Frankie, and listen good. Your lawyer will meet you in Baton Rouge. Until then, Brent and I will be baby-sitting.''

The agent dug the baton even deeper into Frankie's Adam's apple.

Frankie gagged. His bound hands flailed in an attempt to push Stan away, but the cuffs prevented any real leverage.

Brent Caldwell joined his partner, leaning close to whisper, "We've been warned that you've got friends on the outside that are willing to help you. Friends who are far too nosy for their own good. So if you're thinking of doing something stupid, Frankie—*don't.* Stan and I have planned a nice, quiet little trip. If you so much as look at us cross-eyed or flinch when you're not supposed to, we shoot. Understand?''

For one startling instant, Frankie's eyes blazed with the same vitriolic meanness that his lawyer had tried to conceal from the jury during his latest trial. In that unguarded moment, Elizabeth could see that Frankie was well aware of the repercussions awaiting him since being caught and convicted. Frankie had already been sentenced to death row in the Utah State Penitentiary—with the potential for the same punishment in two more states. He had nothing to lose.

Regardless of the FBI agent's warnings, he would do everything in his power to escape.

Stan abruptly released the man and Frankie sagged, propping his hands on his knees and gulping air into his system. As he did so, Stan easily stowed his *coup baton* in the pocket of his trench coat.

When Brent moved to take his arm, Frankie hissed and jerked free. "You'll pay for that," Frankie whispered, pinning his dark gaze on Stan. "You'll both pay for that. If I have to hunt you, and your families, and your friends until the day you die, you'll pay."

"Yeah?" Brent taunted. "Well, first you'll have to get away, won't you?"

Catching the curious stares that were pinned on his passengers, Seth gestured to a door behind them. "I've got a water cooler in my office if you'd like. You could wait in there where it's more...private."

Nodding their thanks, the two men tugged the reluctant convict after them. Even with the none-too-subtle jerk the agents gave Webb's restraints, they couldn't prevent the prisoner from turning one last time and staring at Elizabeth with dark, angry eyes.

Startled, Elizabeth dropped her bags on the floor again. Her stomach suddenly churned. "Where can I—I need a rest room, please."

Seth studied her consideringly, then pointed to a hall several yards away. "Right down there, second door on the right. I'll watch your bags for you."

"Thanks," she offered faintly, nearly running down the appropriate path. Spying the door marked women, she dodged inside. Then, leaning heavily against the panels, she closed her eyes and gulped air into her starving lungs.

Chapter Two

"Gracious!"

Elizabeth's eyes sprang open and she winced. A tall, spare woman with iron-gray hair had witnessed her distress.

"You look as if you've seen a ghost," the woman remarked as she patted a wet paper towel to her face.

Embarrassed, Elizabeth straightened and joined the woman at the wall of mirrors.

"Close," she muttered. "My ex-husband."

The woman's eyes twinkled. "Mmm. Sounds intriguing."

"I assure you, it's not. It's merely…awkward."

"Ahhh." The woman's lips lifted in a wry grin. "Is that why your cheeks are so flushed?"

Darting a glance at her reflection, Elizabeth grimaced. "Damn," she whispered. "I was hoping I'd managed to look calm and collected."

Suddenly weary, Elizabeth planted her hands on either side of the sink and fought a wave of dizziness.

What on earth had possessed her to take five pills? *Five.*

"I know just how you feel," the older woman said, a low chuckle easing from her lips. "My late husband had a way of discombobulating me something fierce, I can tell you."

Elizabeth's lips twitched in amusement. "I don't think I've heard anyone use 'discombobulating' in a sentence before."

The woman shrugged. "A professional hazard, I suppose." She held out her hand. "Willa Hawkes. I'm a librarian."

Elizabeth shook Willa's hand, delighting in the scent of carnations that seemed to hover in the air when Willa moved. Elizabeth's grandmother had worn a similar perfume on special occasions.

"Are you taking the Western Skies charter?" Elizabeth asked.

"Mmm." Willa nodded and bent to gather the carry-on luggage she'd left on the floor. "I'm on my way to Denver for the Overland Exhibit being developed by one of their museums. Several of the diaries from our branch's Originals Department have been requested as part of the display." She patted the leather bag she carried. "There's no way I'd allow a delivery service to take them, so I insisted on flying to Denver myself." She offered Elizabeth a wink. "Of course, a free trip to Colorado and a weekend in a hotel sweetened the pot considerably, I can assure you."

The tinny sound of the public address system interrupted anything more that Willa might have said.

"Passengers for flight 356 to Denver are now requested to board. Please have your tickets ready as you leave the building."

"That's us," Willa said cheerfully. She offered Elizabeth another wink. "Don't take too long. You wouldn't want to miss your flight."

The door bounced quietly behind Willa's back, and Elizabeth was left alone beneath the flickering fluorescent light. For several long moments, she stared at her reflection in the mirror.

She *could* miss her flight. She could barricade herself in the bathroom and never come out.

As soon as the thoughts raced through her head, she pushed them away. She would not regress to adolescence just because she'd met Seth Brody again. She had to remember her job, her responsibilities.

Bending, she splashed cold water on her face and blotted the moisture away with a paper towel. Then, fortifying herself with a deep breath, she marched into the hall.

To her infinite relief, Seth had been detained at the counter. A young, freckle-faced man clutched at his rucksack, his features reflecting a mixture of apprehension and infinite joy.

"I won this contest on the radio, you know. I'm on my way to Aruba," Elizabeth heard him say.

Seth murmured something in response, but Elizabeth quickly ducked away, heading for the snack counter. Perhaps if she had something to drink—coffee, a cola—she'd be able to snap out of her mental fog.

Unfortunately, she found her way barred by a businessman and what appeared to be his secretary.

"Don't forget, Mr. Walsh. The bank auditor will be here first thing Monday morning."

"Thank you, Wendy."

"I've cancelled all your other appointments and rescheduled your tee time."

Walsh didn't appear to be listening. He was studying the snack-stand menu as if it held the secrets to the world. But when the counter attendant asked for his order, he didn't seem to hear.

"Did you reach my wife?" he finally asked.

Sensing that the man wasn't about to order anytime soon, the attendant motioned to Elizabeth.

"No, sir."

"I wanted to…" Walsh sighed.

Sensing the conversation would continue unabated, Elizabeth mouthed "coffee" and held her hands wide apart to signify that she wanted the largest cup the snack counter had.

The teenager scurried to get Elizabeth's order just as Walsh seemed to wake from a fog.

"I'll try to get her on the cell phone. Thanks, Wendy. Have a good weekend."

Obviously dismissed, the woman offered him a smile, then hurried from the terminal, eager to leave before the weather worsened.

"That will be two dollars."

As Elizabeth dug through her purse for her change,

she saw that Walsh was taking an incredibly small cellular phone from his pocket. Time and time again, he tried to dial, swore and then punched the buttons again. But his hands were shaking so badly he couldn't manage to complete the sequence.

Instantly, the man earned Elizabeth's sympathy. It would seem that she wasn't the only person on the plane who was afraid of flying.

The clerk handed her the steaming cup of coffee, and Elizabeth indicated that the girl should make another one.

"Here," she said, handing it to the man named Walsh.

He glanced at her in surprise, so lost in his own world that it was obvious he hadn't seen her until now.

"Coffee," Elizabeth said succinctly.

The man allowed a puff of air to escape his lungs. "Thanks." Taking a sip, he visibly relaxed, then punched the same sequence of numbers he'd tried at least a dozen times before. This time, he was successful in his attempt, but even from where Elizabeth stood, she could hear the tinny, canned voice of an answering machine.

"Damn. I hate these things," Walsh muttered, savagely pushing the end button. "But my wife insisted on having an answering machine so she can screen her calls."

He slid the phone in his pocket, then held out a hand in Elizabeth's direction. "Peter Walsh."

His grip was warm and sure, his hands bearing the neat manicuring of a wealthy executive.

"Elizabeth Boothe."

The clerk returned with the second cup of coffee.

"These are on me," Peter said when Elizabeth would have added to the pile of bills still waiting on the counter. He offered Elizabeth a slight wink. "You're a lifesaver."

Smiling her thanks, Elizabeth collected her coffee and her money, then turned.

And came face-to-face with Seth Brody.

"The runways are cleared and we're beginning final boarding," he said loud enough for Walsh to hear, even though it was obvious that he only meant to speak to Elizabeth.

"Then I'd better hurry."

The man gathered his garment bag and strode away.

Before she could react to being alone with Seth again, her ex-husband grasped her arm.

"Seth, you'd better get going or the storm front we're expecting could make the runways ugly," Patty called from the doorway.

Seth waved to the plump woman, who had returned to hold the fire door for the FBI agents and their prisoner. But his gaze remained on Elizabeth. His fingers closed around her wrist, effectively preventing whatever escape she might make.

"We need to talk, Lizzie."

Lizzie. She'd always detested the derivative of her name.

"I'd like some answers for what happened three years ago," he continued lowly, deliberately.

"I—uh…"

Elizabeth scrambled to make a crushing reply or a witty farewell, but the medication was beginning to kick in, muddling her presence of mind. Only one thought seemed to reverberate with any degree of coherence:

Get out of here. Now. You don't have the time or the energy for a confrontation. Paul will have to handle his own account and his own clients.

But she couldn't run away.

She wouldn't.

"Seth?" Patty prompted again from the door. "You've got to move now."

Seth sighed. "I guess this is neither the time nor the place," he conceded. His scowl intensified. "Yet."

The final word made it plain that he meant to conduct a very pointed interrogation in the none-too-distant future.

Before Elizabeth could form any sort of a coherent reply, Seth had pulled her back to the ticket counter. There he gathered the suit bag and her portfolio case and grasped her elbow.

"This way."

Elizabeth shivered. Every muscle in her body screamed for her to take the opposite direction, to walk out of Seth's life as suddenly as she'd stumbled into it. She didn't need the anxiety of a charter flight on a small jet with a convicted serial murderer. Nor did she need to spend the next few hours as a virtual emotional prisoner of her ex-husband. Under the circumstances, she couldn't possibly endure the hurt, the disillusionment or the tumultuous wonder of entering Seth's life again.

He must have sensed a portion of her thoughts, because he bent close to her ear and whispered, "Chicken."

Damn it. He was always pushing her, challenging her.

While she melted at the mere stroke of his breath against her cheek.

No. She would not let him do this to her. Never again. She was over Seth Brody. She wasn't the weak, naive little nobody who had been so bowled over by the handsome professor from NYU. She'd become a woman in her own right, one with her own aspirations and strength. She would not let him take any of those accomplishments away from her.

Wrenching free from his grip, she yanked her bags from his fingers—strong, slender fingers. Powered by the fuel of her own determination, she marched to the fire door and into the cold.

SETH BRODY HAD TO JOG to catch up with his ex-wife. He'd been expecting Elizabeth to run for the exit, not stomp toward the plane. Even so, as he closed the distance between them, he couldn't fault the view. Entranced, he eyed the grace and sensual twitch of his ex-wife's hips as she strode across the tarmac to the jet.

Regardless of the fact that Lizzie had tried to put as much distance between them as possible, Seth grabbed a fistful of her coat and forced her to stop.

Judging by her militant expression, it was obvious she would have preferred to be anywhere but here. Frankly, Seth couldn't blame her, but that didn't mean he intended to let her have her own way.

Elizabeth Boothe.

The only woman he'd ever married.

The only woman he'd ever...

Loved? How could he even think such a thing after what she'd done to him? Three years ago, he'd dragged himself from the warmth of their bed to drive to a national air show scheduled in Maryland. After traveling for hours and enduring increasingly bad weather, he'd checked with his colleagues and had been informed that the performance was canceled because of high winds from an offshore hurricane.

Turning for home, Seth had spent half a day wending his way through the debris-strewn back roads, fighting slashing rains and gale-force gusts. But he would have done anything to be with her. His wife. To sample her lips once more. To tell her—for the first time aloud—how much he loved her, how he wanted to spend the rest of his life with her.

He'd returned to find their apartment empty of everything that could remotely be considered hers. She hadn't even left the strip of photographs they'd purchased in one of those tacky booths in Atlantic City just after they'd married. Instead, taped to the refrigerator, he'd found a terse note that inspired more questions than answers.

She'd made a mistake.

They were too different.

She had to go.

A tightness gathered in Seth's throat as he stared down at her.

He shouldn't feel anything but anger, hurt—maybe a touch of revenge. But even as he reminded himself that he'd been the one who'd been wronged in their relationship, he couldn't help the way his eyes made a convulsive sweep of her frame.

She didn't look good—and that fact gave him no pleasure. She was thin to the point of being gaunt. The spark of laughter had abandoned her indigo eyes. Tiny lines of tension lined her lips, and her features held a finely etched wariness. The strain he saw wasn't merely the result of their unexpected meeting. The changes were too deeply ingrained.

Lizzie closed her eyes, weaving slightly, and he frowned, pulling her close, supporting her with an arm around her waist. To his infinite surprise, she yawned and melted into him. The cup of coffee she held dropped from her fingers and spilled into the slush.

"Hey, guys! Wait up!" A voice called from the direction of the terminal.

Jerking his attention back to a middle-aged man running toward the plane, Seth nodded to show he'd heard. But Elizabeth's nearness so filled his senses,

he couldn't fathom the reason for the sudden appearance of the stranger.

The portly gentleman wore a parka large enough
for an Arctic expedition, thick, fur-lined gloves, and
boots that Seth's grandmother would have called ga-
loshes. All the while, he struggled with a plaid suit
bag slung over his shoulder and a heavy-sided samples case.

Before Seth could react, the man skidded to a halt,
grabbed Seth's free hand, and pumped it vigorously.

"The name's Richard Brummel, but they call me
Sticky Ricky."

Despite the many eccentric characters who had
flown with Seth—from sight-seeing movie stars to
obnoxiously overpaid sports figures—he'd never
heard anyone actually admit to such a horrendous
nickname.

"I'm a salesman."

Seth had already guessed as much.

"You know those little minibars hotels have in
their rooms? I'm the man who stocks them." He
chuckled. "Well, I don't *actually* stock them, mind
you. The hotel 'help' does that. But I'm the one who
stocks the stockers, mind you."

He guffawed enthusiastically. Then, seeing that
neither Seth nor Elizabeth had responded, he dug into
his pockets.

"Here's a sample on me. Let's see…you look like
a whiskey sort of person." He extended a mini-bottle
in Seth's direction.

Seth stared at the salesman, wondering if he'd lost his mind.

"Maybe not." Ricky snickered, winking. "I don't suppose you're the sort to drink and fly. And being the pilot makes you the ol' designated flier, doesn't it?"

Seth didn't answer. He couldn't. At that moment, Elizabeth had snuggled even closer and her hand had delved inside his coat. As if her arm had suddenly grown too heavy to support, she tucked her fingers beneath his belt and the waistband of his jeans.

Ricky must have sensed that his jokes were falling flat, because he hurriedly offered, "I'll just give a few of these to your little lady. The two of you can have a drink on me later...er, at your leisure."

After dipping into his pocket again, he shoved a handful of mini-bottles, miniature candy bars and peanut packages into the rear pouch of Elizabeth's purse.

"I think you'd better take a seat," Seth said. He sucked in a breath as Elizabeth's fingers wriggled a bit lower inside his waistband. "We've got to get going if we're going to beat the weather."

"Oh. Sure."

Ricky offered Seth another wink before lumbering onto the aircraft, bumping the doorjamb with his samples case as he struggled to make his way inside.

Amid the salesman's loud rendition of apologies— "Pardon me, excuse me"—Seth leaned toward Elizabeth's ear and whispered, "What the hell are you doing?"

"I'm..."

Elizabeth didn't finish, and he waited for the rest of her response.

After a minute, it became clear that she wasn't about to continue at all. In fact, if the entire idea weren't ridiculous for the teetotaling Elizabeth he knew, he'd have said she'd already been nipping into the mini-bottles. Either that or...

Damn. She got airsick. Especially on smaller planes. He'd tried to take her flying only once, in a pre–World War One biplane, and she'd been sicker than a dog the whole time. Afterward, she'd insisted on taking motion-sickness medication whenever they traveled—and she invariably took too much and slept through most of the trip.

As much as Seth regretted dislodging her fingers, he forced Elizabeth to face him.

She stumbled in her efforts to stand under her own power, then offered him a cockeyed grin. That lopsided smile reminded him more than anything else of the woman he'd been willing to marry only a few short days after meeting her.

"How many did you take, Elizabeth?"

"Mmm?" Her gaze was decidedly bleary.

"How many motion-sickness pills?"

She squinted at him in obvious concentration. "Nine."

"Nine!"

Her giggle was positively giddy. "Jus' kidding."

"How many?"

Her brows furrowed. "Three...no...four. Or was it five?"

"Hell. Billy!" He called to the college student who worked part-time loading baggage into the underbelly of Western Skies charter planes.

"Yes, sir?"

"Take these bags as well," Seth said, indicating Lizzie's luggage. Then he bent and lifted Elizabeth into his arms.

Billy's eyes widened at the unaccustomed display of affection from his normally aloof employer. His lips tilted in a way-to-go grin, but he didn't comment other than to say, "Sure, boss. Her purse, too?"

Elizabeth reacted with a bit of her usual spirit, clutching the bag to her chest. "Don't you dare. It's got my mini-bottles."

Billy obviously thought she'd indulged in one mini-bottle too many, but he released his grip on the huge leather bag and carried the others to the rear of the plane.

Seth's jaw was tight as he murmured, "You've got a lot of explaining to do once you're sober, Lizzie. As soon as we land, you and I are going to have a serious talk."

She nodded in mock earnestness. "Very serious. Very, very serious."

Knowing she was in no condition for any kind of rational discussion, Seth climbed the steps to the aircraft and set Elizabeth in the copilot's seat. Then, buckling her in—perhaps a little more tightly than necessary—he stepped outside again to gather the final checklist papers from Billy.

"Will you and Patty be all right until the next shift arrives?" Seth asked as he fastened the forms to the clipboard. "Due to all this bad weather, we've got two planes grounded back East."

"Yeah, sure. What with that new guy you hired, we should—"

Seth stiffened. "What new guy?"

Billy squinted at him, then swept his eyes around the area as if trying to pinpoint the person in question.

"There was some new maintenance guy here about an hour ago. He was cleaning the upholstery." Billy shrugged. "He wasn't one of the two temps we've had lately, so I just assumed he was a new hire."

Seth's brow furrowed. Since he'd lost two of his part-time employees to graduate school, he'd been forced to make do with a temporary service. The temps had checked in with him at the beginning of the shift, so Seth was sure they were the same employees who had been working at the airport all week.

"You're sure it was somebody new?"

Billy shrugged. "Maybe it was a trainee for the temp service. You know how they're always having a new guy tagging along."

"Did you check his work?"

"Sure. He did a real nice job. The plane was clean and ready to go."

Pushing aside his misgivings, Seth made a mental note to talk with the temp agency. He thought he'd made it clear that no unauthorized personnel came in contact with his planes.

No one.

"Have a good trip, Seth."

Seth waved to Billy, stepped back into the jet and fastened the door. Then he slid into his own place with only a brief glance at Liz.

She was asleep.

Or pretending to be asleep. With takeoff only minutes away, he was sure that she was absorbing each scrap of conversation, each smidgen of information being offered by the other passengers. Anything to keep her mind off the moment when they all became airborne.

But he couldn't think about that now. He had a job of his own to do.

Taking a deep breath, Seth closed his eyes and consciously cleared his thoughts of everything but the flight ahead and the departure checklist.

Chapter Three

"It's just a routine flight," Seth had told himself when he'd set Lizzie in the copilot's seat and introduced himself to his other passengers. When the weather suddenly became black and violent, he'd muttered the words under his breath. But when the plane was caught in the downdraft of a wind sheer and Seth struggled for control, everything changed in an instant.

Behind him, he heard the cries of the passengers as the jet seemed to drop from the sky then leapt up again. Still, Seth was able to keep the craft under control right up to the moment when he heard an ominous popping noise. The hydraulic controls became sluggish and he knew they were all in trouble.

Immediately reaching for the radio controls, he ignored the shrieking alarms and fought to bring the plane level. Minutes seemed like hours as his mind raced to figure out a solution to the failing systems and dangerous weather.

"Mayday, mayday, mayday!"

Seth struggled to keep the jet in the air as ice and hail pummeled the windshield and gusts of wind threatened to rip the controls from his hands.

"Mayday, mayday, mayday!"

There was no response to his frantic calls. He'd heard nothing over the headset but static since hitting a micro-cell of sleet and gale-force winds.

Swearing, he gave up on the radio. The unknown force that had damaged his hydraulics had disabled the radio as well. Right now, he had more important worries on his mind—such as keeping the aircraft from dropping like a rock when he had limited flaps and rudder capabilities.

"I want everyone to buckle up as tight as you can!" he shouted to the passengers behind him.

His gaze momentarily flicked away from the array of electronic controls. Even though he willed himself to look at the men and women strapping themselves more tightly into their seats, his eyes caught and held on to the woman who sat in the copilot's seat.

For the first time since Seth had deposited her there, Elizabeth was awake and aware of her surroundings—aware of him. Her eyes were wide and haunted, filled with disbelief. Despite the history between them, she watched him with earnest supplication. She trusted him to make things better, to reassure her that everything was all right.

More than anything, he wanted to tell her that things would be fine. But he couldn't lie to her. Not like this. Not now.

Allowing one last quick look in her direction, he

returned his attention to the controls and said sternly, "Liz, I want you to work your way to one of the rear seats."

"But—"

Ignoring the note of earnest entreaty in that single word, he overrode any objections she might make. The medication she'd taken had made her reactions sluggish, and he could only hope she interpreted a portion of his urgency.

"Just do it. We've lost hydraulic controls to most of the flaps and rudders. We're going down, and we're going down hard. If we're lucky enough to hit a bare patch of snow, we're likely to slide our way to a stop. The nose will take the most damage so the rear of the plane will be safer for you."

He saw the way she struggled to make sense of his instructions amid the shrieking alarms, the whine of the storm and her own drug-clouded consciousness.

The plane hit a pocket of air, dropping like an out-of-control elevator before Seth could right it again. Struggling to pull the plane into low glide, he willed himself to keep his attention on the controls, only the controls. He mustn't entertain half-remembered images of Elizabeth during the happier times they'd shared. He mustn't indulge in thoughts of rumpled bedclothes, breakfasts in bed, long afternoon walks…

He forced his thoughts to the problem at hand. That part of his life was over—and if he didn't keep his wits about him, none of them would have much of a future, either.

"Damn it, Lizzie, get in the back!"

Refusing to meet her gaze, he leaned sideways long enough to release her safety belt. "On your way to the rear of the plane, tell the other passengers to check their safety belts, then remove glasses, jewelry, high heels—anything that could prove potentially dangerous on impact."

Impact.

The word jolted her into action far more quickly than anything he'd said so far. Heeding his instructions, she whipped off her shoes and stuffed them in her oversized purse. Her hands trembled visibly as she struggled to remove delicate diamond stud earrings and an art deco lapel pin. Then, bracing her hands on the seat backs, she swung her legs into the aisle and fought for balance.

Seth yanked his attention back to the windshield in front of him as Elizabeth stood in the archway leading to the rest of the plane and shouted to the passengers, "Take off anything sharp or fragile and stow it in your carry-on luggage—jewelry, glasses, anything that could break on impact."

Good girl, Seth silently congratulated her. Her voice held a note of command that quieted the shouts of the passengers. She offered them all something to do—no matter how trivial their efforts might be in the long run—to help them feel a little less helpless, a little less doomed.

"Come on, come on!" she shouted. "If you don't

have a place to stow your gear, put it in my bag. Let's go, let's go!''

The plane veered wildly and Lizzie stumbled, falling against Seth, her hand gripping his shoulder.

Seth sucked in his breath. For one brief moment, he remembered the way that hand had once felt against bare skin.

Was this what happened in the moments before a person was about to die? Was his life flashing before his eyes?

No. Not his life.

His life with Elizabeth.

At that moment, the plane tore through the storm clouds. In the hazy half-light, he could see the craggy summits of the Rockies, and there, in the distance, a pristine snow-covered clearing.

Without conscious thought, he reached to squeeze her fingers.

"Get in the back, Lizzie. We're going down. Now."

THE STARK FINALITY in Seth's tone was enough to spur Elizabeth into action. Bracing her feet as firmly as possible on the carpeted aisle, she clung to the seat backs, making her way down the aisle, automatically checking the other passengers and stowing their belongings as she went.

But her mind was a million miles away, a million years away. She was at the seaside wedding of a friend and a breeze was trying to rip the flower from her hair when a deep voice inquired, *"Need some help?"*

Seth Brody.

He'd stormed into her life with all the subtlety of a bulldozer. One week later, she'd been signing her name next to his on a marriage certificate. Her colleagues and friends had thought her decision completely irresponsible and impetuous—and therefore so unlike her. Elizabeth had always been so pragmatic, so pedantic, so in control.

But Seth had taken her breath away. He'd brought joy and adventure to her life—so much so, that her heart beat faster at the mere thought of him. Their passion had been overwhelming, their attraction instantaneous.

Was it any wonder their marriage had self-destructed so quickly?

The thought brought a wave of loss more powerful than anything Elizabeth had felt in a long time.

A gasp tore from her throat as the plane suddenly lurched into a plunging dive and the aisle threatened to become a slippery incline of gray carpet.

Summoning what little strength she had left, she lunged into the last empty passenger seat and scrambled to fasten the safety belt around her waist.

The plane dropped sharply, righted itself, then dropped again, causing even the hardened, implacable FBI agents seated in front of her to cry out.

"Brace yourselves!" she heard Seth shout.

Sobbing, she tried to make sense of the strap and

buckle and metal with fingers that had grown suddenly foreign and disobedient.

"Don't do this to me," she begged in a choked voice as she finally managed to slide the tongue of one strap into the buckle of the other. In the confusion, she'd jammed part of her jacket into the mechanism and the clasp refused to lock.

Fighting the fabric, the buckle and her own panic, she glanced around her, feeling suddenly very alone and more frightened than she would have thought possible. The other passengers had bent to wrap their arms over their heads so she had an unobstructed view to the front of the plane—of Seth, and the expanse of snow rushing to meet them.

"Dear God," she whispered as the wind-driven flurries cleared and a jagged outcrop of rock suddenly appeared to one side. In a sickening, distorted montage, the ground hurtled toward them. A blur of white and steel blue raced past the window.

"Hold on!"

Even as Seth shouted the warning, the plane hit the snow with a sickening jolt, bounced, then hit again, again. The wild shriek of grinding snow, cracking glass, screeching metal filled Elizabeth's ears. The sharp, bitter taste of her own blood filled her mouth as her teeth sank into her lip. Then, she crumpled forward, her body slamming against the seat in front of her before being thrown to the floor where she was wedged into the space between the rows. Crying out, she attempted to fold herself into a protective fetal ball, her arms wrapping over her head as luggage and wreckage flew through the air, bombarding her with debris.

"Seth!"

The garbled scream was swallowed by awful, enveloping blackness.

SETH GRUNTED in pain, his lungs swelling with a deep, ragged breath.

He was alive.

Wasn't he?

A groan lodged in his throat and he fought against the darkness that threatened to swamp him. No. He had to hang on. He couldn't let himself be pulled under. He had to think. Remember.

Bit by bit, moment by excruciating moment, he became aware of himself, of his body still pressing against the strap of his safety belt, the chill wetness of snow against his fingers.

Alive. He had to be alive, he finally decided. Death couldn't possibly require this much effort.

His head pounded, and his eyes squeezed tightly shut in an effort to drown out the haunting images of the crash. But his brain seemed caught in an endless loop, reliving the jarring impact of the underbelly hitting snow, the skidding, sliding, out-of-control landing, the squeal of the wing tearing loose, the screams of the passengers.

Then the awful, echoing silence.

Passengers.

He had to see to his passengers.

Automatically, his mind latched on to the responsibilities that awaited him. He took a bracing gulp of air, then lifted his drooping head and forced his eyes open.

Gradually, the web of cracked safety glass came into focus. Seth blinked, wondering if his sight had been compromised when the world beyond seemed to be shrouded in some bizarre opaque fog. It took several minutes before he realized that the nose of the plane had dug into the drifts, throwing snow over the windshield.

Snow.

There was snow inside too. Glancing to his right, he noted that a tree branch had pierced the far corner of the glass, torn the control panel apart and sent a shower of snow over the copilot's seat.

Not a pretty landing, but a landing nonetheless, he decided.

Closing his eyes again, Seth allowed the pounding of his own pulse to thrum through his body. Bit by bit, most of the pain began to ease into a weary ache. The stabbing pressure that remained was centered at a spot over his right eye.

Gingerly, he touched the spot, then hissed when his fingertips were bathed in the warmth of his own blood.

First-aid box. He needed to find the first-aid box.

But try as he might to summon the wherewithal to stand, to move, to *think,* he seemed to be locked in limbo. For several long, infinitely satisfying moments, it was enough to sit still, absorb the silence and revel in the miracle of air filling his lungs.

He was alive.

Reluctantly, he was forced to acknowledge that if the plane had landed a little more to the left, or if the protruding branch had been a few feet more to his side of the plane...

The branch.

Copilot seat.

Lizzie.

The memory of who had vacated the seat to his right slammed into his consciousness, bringing with it the image of his ex-wife, her eyes wide and pleading as she fought to make her way to the rear of the plane.

Gritting his teeth, Seth slid his palm across his hips until he located the clasp to his safety belt. A stain of fresh blood left a perfect fingerprint on the metal of the buckle, but he paid no heed to the evidence of his own mortality. He wasn't the only person in the jet. There had been nine passengers and himself.

The soft snap of the belt ricocheted through the silence that blanketed the marooned aircraft. A low grunt lodged deep in Seth's throat as the sound caused an echo of ripping metal to reverberate in his brain. Without thinking, he shook his head to rid it of the phantom noises, then groaned when a blinding burst of pain exploded behind his eye.

"Damn," he muttered aloud.

Don't think about it now. Don't think about the cold seeping into your joints or the icy dampness coating the controls, or the bumps and bruises clamoring for attention.

Bringing the plane down to earth had been the first major obstacle on this ill-fated journey, but he still had work to do.

Filling his lungs with a bracing draft of air, Seth swung his legs free, pushed himself to his feet and locked his elbows to prop himself upright. But as he looked toward the area that had once been the rear of his finest plane, his blood turned to ice. A horror like nothing he'd ever known before flooded his limbs.

Dear God in heaven. How could anyone else have survived?

Even in the near darkness, Seth was able to see that the bulk of the plane had split into three pieces in the wintry clearing. Beyond the cockpit, a huge trough of snow marked the path the separate parts had taken—from the initial impact, to the skidding stop.

Fifty feet away, the bulk of the fuselage had come to rest, the tail and rudder poking out of the drifts of snow like the broken wing of a bird. To the right, one wing had sheared off, then, judging by the displaced snow, it had cartwheeled end over end before coming to rest against a rocky bluff a hundred yards away. In its wake were blotches made by engine parts, luggage, seats, and chunks of upholstery.

On the fringes of his gaze, Seth noted one of the FBI agents limping toward a spot where a pair of chairs had been thrown into a snowbank. Other smaller sections of the wreckage had also been cast willy-nilly over the clearing, and to his relief, Seth saw flashes of movement, life.

But...where was Elizabeth?

Renewing his study of the damage, he noted that the tail section and the largest portion of the jet had remained intact, creating an eerie cross-section view of the interior of his newest and largest plane. Lizzie had tried to reach the rear of the aircraft, so she must still be there.

Without warning, an explosion rocked the valley, making the ground shudder beneath Seth's feet. Automatically, he ducked, shielding his face as the shattered wing section burst into flames.

The roar of the fire rumbled over the clearing, filling his ears. An eerie bloodred light illuminated the wreckage with horrifying clarity. A blast of heat rolled over him, then subsided in the gust of a numbing wind.

"Liz!"

Seth wasn't aware of shouting her name out loud. He only knew that he had to find her, make sure she had survived.

A burst of adrenaline pushed away the aches of his body. Seth lunged beneath exposed cables and dangling wires, stumbling into the snow, righting himself, then wading through knee-high powder.

"Elizabeth!" There was no response to his call, no flutter of movement from the interior of the plane.

Then again, he comforted himself, the storm and the angle of the fire had caused the fuselage to be cloaked in shadows. Even the wind kicked up puffs of snow, obscuring his view.

"Help me! Over here! I'm caught!"

Seth veered toward the FBI agent he'd seen moments ago, following the frantic voice, catching sight of a splash of orange.

"I'm going to burn. Please, please, you've got to get me out of here. I can't move."

Seth's work boots fought for traction as he and another passenger raced to the voice. Glancing at the man who half limped, half ran to help, Seth recognized one of the FBI agents who'd shown his credentials at the airport. Stan. Wasn't that the man's name? Stan Kowalski?

"Give me a hand," Seth shouted over the roar of the fire.

He and Stan tugged at a long strip of metal which had been torn from the outer shell of the plane until Frankie Webb was able to kick free and roll out of the way. The convict lay quivering, his face pressed into the snow.

"Please, you've got to take the cuffs off. Please."

Stan sighed, regarded the leg chains and finally relented.

"Don't get any ideas, Webb. You've got nowhere to run and no one to help you."

"I'm not going anywhere. Please, just let me loose."

Stan sighed and removed a key from his pocket. He released his feet and one of Frankie's wrists, but kept the other hooked to the man's waist restraint.

"That's as good as it's going to get, Frankie."

Webb used his free hand to push himself into a sitting position, then sat hunched in the snow, sobbing.

Seth stared at the convict. At the airport, Webb had been so cocky and sure of himself, cold and cruelly calculating. But the near-death experience had clearly shaken him up.

Seth turned his attention to the FBI agent. "Are you all right?"

The man nodded.

"You're limping," Seth pointed out when the man didn't draw attention to the injury.

"I've cut my thigh, but I'll be fine. Go find the others."

Seth hesitated, but Kowalski jerked his head toward the wreckage behind them. "Go on, now. I'll put this one to work as soon as he blows his nose," he added in disgust.

With each step he took toward the shattered plane, Seth's brain grew clearer. Survival skills gleaned from years of working in the outdoors and a stint with one of the local ski patrols kicked into gear.

Before what light the fire provided completely failed, he needed to locate the first-aid kit and the bright orange duffel bag packed with emergency equipment. There should be a flashlight…

He'd have to ration its use.

…emergency beacon…

Was it working?

…warmth…shelter…

How low would temperatures drop tonight?

A fresh spurt of energy hit his system as he reached the shattered mouth of the aircraft. A figure stood in the yawning opening—a feminine form.

For a moment, Seth dared to hope that Elizabeth had come to meet him halfway, but he instantly discounted the idea since the shape was older and plumper.

His mind was working more clearly now, and he remembered the roster of passengers that he'd surveyed mere hours earlier. There had been only one female passenger other than the "unknown" party registered through Radon Advertising.

"Mrs. Hawkes?" he said softly, praying that he'd remembered correctly.

The woman blinked at him, her eyes wide and unfocused. "I need to get out of here."

She moved as if to jump into the snow, but Seth stopped her.

"Mrs. Hawkes, I think you should sit down. You should stay inside where it's a little warmer."

"No. I…need to get out of here."

The woman's voice was firm but held an edge of hysteria, so Seth relented, helping to lift her from the wreckage.

Once her feet were on solid ground again, she sank to her knees in the snow and began to sob.

"Ken? Where's Ken?"

Seth's brow furrowed. He was sure that there had been no one by that name on the flight manifest.

"Who's Ken, Mrs. Hawkes?"

She regarded him pleadingly. "My husband. Have you seen my husband? He wouldn't leave me here alone like this. He always takes care of me."

Seth knelt close to her and took her hands. "You were traveling alone, Mrs. Hawkes."

Her expression clearly revealed her confusion. "No. I never travel by myself. I don't like being alone…or…" Her eyes filled with tears. "My books. Where are my books?"

"What books, Mrs. Hawkes?"

"I wouldn't journey across the plains without my…books."

Seth was torn, knowing that he needed to search for other survivors. But how could he leave Willa Hawkes alone in such a state?

"I'll stay with her," a voice said from behind.

Seth whirled to discover Ricky Brummel limping toward him.

"I…I was thrown from the wreckage," Ricky said with a grin that was filled with wonder and stunned disbelief.

"Are you injured?"

"I banged my knee on something, but I'm okay. If anyone asks, I'll just tell them it's an old football injury."

A bark of relieved laughter burst from Seth's throat.

"Go on," Ricky urged, gesturing to the plane. "I think most of us are okay. There's a passenger—a nerdy kind of kid really—puttering around on the other side of the plane, and a guy in a long coat, and another gentleman who crawled out of the plane before the explosion.''

Frantically, Seth tried to assimilate the information. Kowalski and his prisoner. Willa Hawkes, Ricky Brummel and three other men. That left only Elizabeth and another man to account for.

Seth heaved himself into the shattered plane and squinted in an effort to see into the shadows.

''Elizabeth!'' he called. ''Answer me, damn it.''

When he received no response, his gut tightened in dread. What would he do if she weren't part of his life anymore, if…

But she's not part of your life. You're divorced.

True. But until now, he hadn't realized how he'd harbored the possibility of contacting her again, just to see if the sparks still flew….

Sparks.

Light.

Relying on his sense of touch and familiarity, Seth felt his way to the overhead luggage compartment located above the center emergency exit. The door opened with a reluctant squeak—and even with the care he took, he was bombarded with coats and bags.

Ignoring the flotsam, he dug to the rear of the bin where a plastic tackle box filled with first-aid supplies had been strapped to the bulkhead. Yanking the cover open, he blindly felt for a pair of plastic cylindrical tubes.

Bull's-eye.

Breaking the seal on one tube, he shook the liquid

inside and a bright greenish light glowed, caught, then blazed, illuminating the interior.

Frantically, his eyes swept the wreckage. His throat tightened when the plane seemed completely empty of passengers. Then, he caught a glimpse of a slim hand that stretched into the aisle from the space between the last two seats on the opposite side.

"Lizzie?" he whispered. He began tossing bags and coats aside so that he could hunker in the aisle.

Somehow, she'd been wedged into a tight ball between the last two seats on the left-hand side of the plane. Her back was wedged against the fuselage, her legs drawn against her body, her head and arm half-resting on her seat.

Hesitantly, he reached to brush a strand of hair away from the face. The long, silky tresses clung to the blood on his fingers. Fearfully, he tucked his hand beneath her jaw, searching for a pulse. His own heart slammed against the wall of his chest when he felt the flutter of life.

"Elizabeth," he murmured, smoothing the hair away from her cheek, praying that her eyelids would open. A limp seat belt swayed mockingly from the edge of the cushion.

"Why didn't you fasten yourself in?" he whispered.

Beads of sweat formed on his upper lip as her body remained unresponsive. A surge of protectiveness rose in his throat, blocking his ability to breathe properly.

She looked so helpless, so vulnerable—qualities

he doubted had ever been attributed to Elizabeth Boothe. In her business and professional life, she offered such an indomitable aura that there was no doubt in anyone's mind that she was a woman in control. She rarely asked for help, let alone displayed any form of need. Even with him. Despite their passionate relationship and the vows they'd exchanged, Elizabeth had never needed him.

Seth held his breath when he thought he detected a slight quivering sigh.

He cupped her cheek, burying his fingers in the ebony cloud of hair. Other than that single gesture of comfort, he didn't dare move her until she regained consciousness.

"Elizabeth, I want you to tell me where you're hurt," he commanded softly, bending close so that the cloud caused by his breath skimmed her cheek. "Elizabeth, answer me."

Finally, a soft, kittenlike whimper eased from her throat and her lashes flickered.

"That's it, sweetheart. Come back to me."

Chapter Four

That's it, sweetheart. Come back to me.

The gruff, strangely familiar tones pulled Elizabeth from a deep, warm cocoon.

She knew that voice. That endearment.

But who?

Come back to me. Come back...

In an instant, she was yanked from the warm, velvety safety of her emotional hiding place.

"No," she whispered, beginning to tremble. The ground beneath her seemed to shudder and shake. The squeal of metal on snow filled her ears. "No! Stop!"

"Elizabeth, open your eyes."

The demanding tones brought everything back to her.

Seth.

The plane.

The accident.

Her lashes sprang open and she focused on a topsy-turvy world of red and greenish lights and shadows, incomprehensible shapes and chaos.

"Am I in hell?" she whispered.

A sound that was half chuckle, half sigh met her ears just as an all-too-familiar face swam into view above her.

"If so, we're both there together. But in my opinion, it's too damned cold to be anything but real life."

Seth. His voice. His strength. She was drawn to him even now, even when she told herself that their life together was irrevocably over.

Her eyes narrowed as she studied the craggy outlines of Seth's jaw, the waves of his hair.

Older. He looked older. But good. So good.

Come back to me.

The words echoed in her brain and she wondered if Seth had actually uttered them or if the plea was a product of her imagination.

Knowing that to pursue such a line of thought could only lead to trouble, Elizabeth struggled to push herself upright.

"Can you help me?" she finally asked when it became obvious that she was hopelessly tangled in coats, blankets and wreckage.

"How badly are you hurt? Any numbness? Loss of feeling?"

Elizabeth wiggled her toes, smiling faintly when they responded to her command. She was cold and battered, but definitely alive. "No problem. I can feel every inch of my body." Wincing, she added, "Trust me. As for any numbness, my toes are freezing, but nothing else seems to be damaged."

Large, broad hands eased under her shoulders and

Seth awkwardly lifted her against his chest. In doing so, he stumbled slightly, pulling her tightly against his body. She had a fleeting impression of lean muscle and bone before he set her down on the seat.

An involuntary moan slipped from her throat as the blood pounded against her skull. Dizziness swept through her, bringing an answering wave of nausea.

"Lizzie?"

Seth's voice seemed to come to her from a long distance, and she fought the encroaching blackness.

"What's wrong?"

She clung to the sound of Seth's voice, the potency of his presence.

"I must have hit my head," she whispered, tentatively lifting her hands to probe beneath her hair. But her fingers shook and her body began to tremble violently.

Seeing her predicament, Seth swiped his hands down his jeans to rid them of the last traces of his own blood. Gathering two of the thin blankets that bore the Western Skies logo, he wrapped them around her shoulders before tipping her face up to his inspection.

"Let me have a look. Then, we'll find your shoes and you can put your feet up. I don't want you going into shock."

She wanted to argue, to insist that she didn't need to be coddled, but at that moment she yearned for the comfort of another person's touch. Seth's touch.

Seth tilted her chin and stared into her eyes—and she prayed she didn't look as hellish as she felt. If she did, there was no evidence in his expression as his broad, callused hands probed her hairline, then delved farther beneath the tangled tresses.

A shaft of pain shot through her skull and down her neck. Elizabeth hissed.

"You've got quite a goose egg already. But considering you didn't fasten your seat belt, it's a wonder you didn't break your neck," Seth commented.

Abandoning the tender area, he continued his search of her head and shoulders.

Elizabeth shivered, and not with the cold. It had been so long since a man had touched her. Indeed, she didn't think she'd allowed anyone close to her since she'd left Seth. She hadn't wanted anyone else.

Unable to stop herself, she reached for the gash curving around his eye. Although she fought against it, the evidence of his own brush with death caused a shuddering awareness to spread through her body.

"You're lucky," she murmured. "One more inch and you could have been blinded."

He shrugged the injury away. "I'll live."

Their eyes met and a tangle of emotions bound them together. They'd survived. They were alive.

"Why did you leave me?" Seth asked, the question uttered so softly, that she nearly didn't hear it as the glowing greenish light grew dimmer and dimmer, then disappeared altogether.

Liz heard Seth swear, felt him shift in the darkness. Then a streak of fluorescent light gathered around them again.

For several long moments, Elizabeth stared up at the only man she'd ever trusted enough to share her life. She'd trusted him enough to make love with him—to *marry* him.

Where had it all gone wrong?

There was no time to analyze the past or their current situation. Before Elizabeth could organize her own thoughts, a scream of pure horror shattered the winter stillness.

Seth was the first to react.

He yanked at the door of a small closet located next to the lavatory in the rear of the plane. The frame had bent during impact, jamming the portal closed.

Hissing an epithet, Seth braced his back against the opposite bulkhead and slammed the bottom of his foot into the offending door. The flimsy barrier broke and sagged inward, allowing a glimpse of coats and luggage.

Kneeling, Seth fumbled in the shadows until he managed to retrieve a bright orange duffel bag from somewhere inside. Then, as the greenish glow of the glo-stick ebbed, he withdrew a huge flashlight and snapped the battery into place.

The white beam was startling in the gloom, further revealing the chaos around them. Elizabeth took a hissing breath, wondering how any of them had managed to survive.

"I'll be right back," Seth said.

Without waiting to hear the objections forming on her tongue, he jumped into the snow and disappeared from view.

The screams came again, horrible, high-pitched sounds of terror.

Elizabeth stumbled to her feet and shivered as the cold, the dark and the unknown threat waiting outside threatened to swamp the few shreds of calm she'd been able to gather together. Barefoot and aching, she felt inordinately vulnerable and mortal.

Since the glo-stick was already beginning to wane, Elizabeth used the sickly light to locate her purse. Because the bag had been tucked under the seat in front of her and her own body had kept it from shifting, it was relatively easy to find. Within seconds, she'd grabbed the athletic shoes she kept in the bottom as well as the thick socks she used to protect her hosiery.

A sigh of delight whispered over her lips as the thick, fleecy fabric hugged her chilled flesh. But she had little time to enjoy the sensation as the screams increased in pitch and volume. Hurrying as quickly as her bruised body would allow, she jammed her feet into the shoes and tugged the laces into place.

Gingerly she stood, closing her eyes when the world around her careened and her knees threatened to collapse.

"Buck up, Elizabeth, buck up," she whispered to herself.

Once her vision had cleared, she reached for the tackle box labeled First Aid. From experience, she knew that Seth would be irritated if she dared to disobey his edicts. But surely he couldn't complain if she brought him the kit.

Although her limbs trembled in reaction, Elizabeth forced herself to walk to the yawning opening. What little light the glo-stick offered had become useless so she tossed it into the snow and stared in horror at the devastation.

Somehow, despite the evidence of the severed aircraft, Elizabeth had expected to see a plane—a damaged plane, a battered plane, but something distantly recognizable as the aircraft she'd boarded in Salt Lake City. Instead, she was met with the sight of bits and pieces of engine parts, seats, torn metal, tangled cables, scattered luggage and the still-smoldering remains of a wing.

Another scream ripped through the night, and Elizabeth started, her eyes automatically searching for the source of the noise. Yards away, Seth was slogging through the snow, heading for the knot of people huddled around a mass of luggage and wreckage.

As he drew closer, the wild arc of the flashlight he held swung to illuminate the horrifying tableau of a male figure. He was still trapped in the confines of his leather seat, but his face was a mass of scarlet, his clothes torn and all but unrecognizable. Wide eyes gazed sightlessly at the sky.

A few feet away, a middle-aged woman stared at the body, her face contorted with fear, her body shaking as she screamed in horror at the sight.

Willa Hawkes. Elizabeth remembered speaking to her in the terminal rest room.

"That guy was in the seat in front of me."

Elizabeth started when a gangly boy-man stepped away from the shadows below her. Belatedly, she realized that this was the passenger who had won a trip to Aruba from a local radio station.

She shivered. None of them would be making their

connecting flights or their excursions into Denver. The night was growing blacker, the fire from the wing dying, snow beginning to fall. Soon, visibility would be all but nil. Any sort of rescue would not be coming until daylight.

"We were both seated near the wing," whispered the gaunt-cheeked passenger. "I was just...behind him. He was one of the...FBI agents. I saw him...when the wing tore loose...saw him...fly out as if..."

Elizabeth didn't want to hear any more. She didn't want to admit that the crash had claimed a fatality. She didn't want to acknowledge how close they'd all come to such a frightful death. She didn't want to remember the way that this man had been cocky, alive and sure of himself when he'd shown his identification to Seth mere moments before they all departed Salt Lake City.

A muffled pop erupted in the night and Elizabeth jumped. She saw the beam of the flashlight whirl as Seth dived into the snow then rolled onto his stomach. Then, farther away, she caught a glimpse of the second FBI agent as he cursed and shouted. Sure that her mind was playing tricks on her, she watched Kowalski aim his pistol at a swiftly fleeing figure dressed in a bright orange jumpsuit and a flimsy denim jacket.

"Get back here, damn you!" the agent yelled, but the fugitive dodged into a copse of trees and disappeared from view.

The agent attempted to follow, but it was clear

from the way he dragged his left leg that he'd been injured.

Seth lunged to his feet and raced to Kowalski's side just as the man collapsed into the snow. Even then, the man rolled to his stomach and continued to shoot wildly into the trees.

"Have you lost your mind?" Seth barked as he yanked the pistol from the lawman's hands.

Kowalski struggled to rise, then fought to crawl forward before finally collapsing in the snow.

"Enough," Seth said, the tone of command carrying to Elizabeth even from this distance. "Let him run. He can't go far. The cold will force him back soon enough."

Elizabeth jumped to the ground. Ignoring the fiery tattoo that knocked at her temples, she forced herself to move. She fought to make her way through the deep snow, keeping to the path that Seth had made to save herself as much effort as possible.

She reached Seth just as Kowalski rolled to his back. He writhed in pain, blood streaming from a long gash in his thigh.

"I brought the first-aid kit," she said to Seth—more to announce her presence than to state the obvious.

Seth shot her a grateful smile. "Good girl." His hands were already ripping at the lawman's trousers so that he could examine the wound. "There should be a set of tweezers, bandages and some gauze pads in a sterile package. See if you can find them."

Sinking into one of the drifts, Elizabeth did as

she'd been told, locating the required items immediately.

Seth took the sterile pack and tore open the pouch with his teeth, then removed the tweezers before tossing the remaining items into the open kit.

"He's got glass and metal embedded in his leg. We'll need to apply pressure to the wound, but I don't dare do anything until we've removed the shrapnel. Can you hold the light for me?"

She nodded, lifting the flashlight and shining it on the agent's thigh. The gash was deep, nearly to the bone, and was peppered with debris from the plane.

The agent's skin grew ashen at the sight. Hoping to distract him, she knelt at the man's side, holding the flashlight in a manner she hoped would block at least a portion of his view.

"What's your name?" she said, nudging him with her knee when he didn't respond.

It was obvious that he knew she was trying to divert his attention, since he'd introduced himself at the airport. But he licked his lips, then looked up at her with steel-gray eyes. "Stan Kowalski."

"You're not a very good shot, Stan."

He gave an involuntary bark of laughter. "Hell, if I'm not. I've got a marksman medal at home."

Her brow arched in patent disbelief, and he quickly said, "It's damn cold and my hands were shaking."

She did her best to offer him a teasing smile. "Somehow I don't think your supervisor will fall for that excuse."

"Screw him."

She laughed. "I hate to break the news, but I'm pretty sure you didn't even wing your prisoner, let alone slow him down."

Stan grimaced, his face twisting with something more than pain.

"Normally, I'd send my partner after him." At that, Stan hissed—though whether from her remark, or Seth's probing, she couldn't tell. "My partner's dead, you know. That's him in the wreckage."

Even Seth looked up. A hush settled over the figures that had gathered close.

"He was thrown free of the plane when the wing sheared off," Stan stated, his voice gruff, flat, hollow. "He landed on nothing but twisted metal and glass—part of the bulkhead, I think."

His voice quavered. "He was alive when I got to him—alive and swearing up a storm. I tried to get him out of his seat, but his belt was all twisted, so I went to find something to cut him loose. That's when I got tangled up in some baggage and fell. Then Frankie jumped me, stole my cuff keys...."

The big man's chin quivered, and Elizabeth felt her own emotions growing shaky.

"My thigh was already beat up from the landing. B-but wouldn't you know it? I cut my damned leg all over again trying to chase that bastard Frankie Webb."

The clearing grew silent. Elizabeth watched as Seth's gaze leapt to the other passengers, and she could all but hear the way he made a mental tally in his head.

Ten people had boarded the plane to Denver. Nine had survived. Several were injured.

And one serial killer had fled into the forest.

Elizabeth found herself studying the survivors in the same way Seth must see them. Willa Hawkes had stopped her screaming and now stood several yards away with her purse clutched to her chest. Obviously suffering from the effects of shock, she kept muttering, "My books, my books, my books…"

Seeing her predicament, Ricky loped toward her and threw an arm around her shoulders.

"Come on, Miss…"

The woman stared at him blankly for a moment, but when Ricky grinned in encouragement, she supplied hoarsely, "Mrs. Hawkes."

"Well then, Mrs. Hawkes. Let's go find your coat."

"Get her as warm as possible, Ricky. Then make her lie down and get her feet up."

Ricky nodded to show he'd heard. Gently, he led Willa to the relative shelter of the shattered tail section. She balked when it was clear that Ricky meant for her to climb inside, but when he would not be dissuaded, she sagged and surrendered to his urgings.

"You there," Seth called, pointing to the haggard businessman who had slumped into one of the seats planted in a nearby drift. Elizabeth recognized him as the man who had bought her coffee in Salt Lake City.

Walsh's eyes clung to Kowalski's gaping wound. "What's your name?" Seth asked.

"Walsh." The man cleared his throat and said more loudly, "Peter Walsh."

"Are you hurt?"

Walsh shook his head, but judging by the way he cradled his arm against his chest, he was offering them a noble front.

"I'll check you over in a minute," Seth said. "What about you?"

He pointed to the last passenger, a tall, cadaverous-looking businessman dressed in a severe black suit and topcoat.

"I'm sure I've got whiplash—probably worse. What the hell happened?"

Elizabeth started, stunned by the pure anger vibrating from the man's voice. Vaguely, she remembered seeing the man seated in the back of the plane just before they'd crashed. Since she hadn't seen him in the terminal, he must have boarded before she arrived.

"I think you owe us all an explanation," the man snapped, directing vitriolic eyes at Seth.

Seth remained calm and unfazed. "We'll discuss all that later. Right now we need to get organized, Mr...."

"Gallegher. Ernst Gallegher. I'm the CEO of Gallegher Enterprises."

The statement was made as if such information was supposed to impress them.

"Mr. Gallegher, Mr. Walsh, I want both of you to head back to the plane as well. All of you should buddy up in the seats or on the floor, then wrap yourselves in blankets to keep warm."

Elizabeth doubted that Peter Walsh had assimilated much of what Seth had said. But when Seth glared at Ernst Gallegher, the man stooped to help Walsh stand. The pair of them staggered after the other retreating figures.

"Hey!" Seth called to the last passenger to be questioned—the same nerdy-looking passenger who had startled Elizabeth earlier. The boy-man was sifting disconsolately through the wreckage, his eyes moist with unabashed tears. "Are you hurt?"

The young man started, then shook his head. "My coat," he said faintly. "I'm trying to find my coat. It's one of those long, wool things. It's really warm. I took it off and shoved it into my carry-on bag." His eyes brightened. "Have you seen it? My bag? It has a brass tag with my name, Michael Nealy."

Elizabeth didn't know how Nealy expected to find anything in the blackness that had begun to descend over the valley. Even the glow of the burned-out wing wasn't providing much light.

"Go join the others, Nealy," Seth bluntly ordered.

"But it's really important that I—"

"Go! And round up any blankets or luggage you find on your way, but I want you in the plane within a minute, understand?"

"But—"

"Damn it, the prisoner who escaped was a serial killer—and since he may have taken a pistol from the dead FBI agent, you probably don't want to be out in the open, do you?"

Elizabeth watched Nealy all but run for the plane.

"Do you really think Frankie Webb will shoot at

us?'' Elizabeth asked nervously, eyeing the darker shadow of the trees.

"Hell, no. I'd bet money that Caldwell's pistol is still in his shoulder holster.''

"Then why—"

"Why'd I say that?'' Seth returned his attention to the injured Kowalski. "I had to get Nealy back to the plane. People in shock do crazy things. If I hadn't motivated him into changing his mind, he probably would have spent the better part of the night looking for his luggage and freezing to death in the process.''

As Seth began to apply tentative pressure to Stan's leg, Elizabeth turned to the FBI agent to offer more inconsequential chitchat to divert his attention. But it was clear to see her efforts at comforting Kowalski would be in vain.

Chapter Five

"Is he dead?" Elizabeth whispered.

Seth checked the pulse point on the man's neck.

"No. He passed out, that's all." Seth's fingers were slick with blood as he pointed to the package he'd thrown into the tackle box. "Hand me those pads, then tear off some long strips of adhesive tape, will you?"

She did as she was told, watching in amazement as Seth skillfully applied pressure to stop the bleeding, then wrapped and secured the wound with tape.

"That should hold him until some proper help gets here," he offered.

Elizabeth latched onto the words "proper help."

"When?" she breathed.

He grew still, immediately interpreting her blunt query.

Squinting up at the sky, he said, "Switch off the light to save the battery. I want to give Kowalski's wound a few more minutes before we try to move him."

Elizabeth hit the button, then sat shivering, staring at Seth's indistinguishable form.

What time was it? Ten? Eleven?

But as quickly as the possibilities occurred to her, she rejected them. The combination of the storm and winter's early sunsets made the night incredibly black. She doubted if more than an hour or two had elapsed since they left Salt Lake City.

"When can we expect some help?" she asked again. Now that the rest of the passengers had returned to the plane, she felt exposed and alone in the snowy field. Despite Seth's reassurances that Frankie Webb wouldn't try anything, the hairs at the back of her neck prickled as if she were being watched.

Seth sighed, slowly admitting, "We lost radio contact before we went down. I'd bet that whatever caused our hydraulics to malfunction destroyed our communications as well."

"There's no chance of fixing it?"

"Not with the damage caused on impact. A tree finished off most of the control panel." He paused before adding, "If you'd been in the copilot's seat, it would have killed you."

She wrapped her arms around her waist, shivering. Thankfully, Seth continued, keeping her from dwelling on the morbid possibilities.

"A flight path was filed before we left, but it will be a few hours yet before we were scheduled to land in Denver." Seth began washing his hands with snow. "Once my employees realize something is wrong, they'll notify the authorities. Until then, we wait.''

Elizabeth wrapped her arms around her chest, shivering as much from fear as the cold.

''How will they find us?''

''There's an emergency beacon in the tail section. Since that part of the plane sustained the least amount of damage, we can hope the equipment is working. If it is, we're already sending out a tracking signal.''

''And if it didn't survive?''

''Don't borrow trouble before we have to. Tomorrow, once the sun's up, I'll have a look at the transmitter and make sure it's functioning properly. There's an access panel near the rudder. But until I've got some light, I doubt I could find the mechanism, let alone do any troubleshooting.''

Which meant that unless the beacon was already emitting its signal, there would be no hope of rescue until morning or midafternoon.

''What do we do in the meantime?''

''Keep as warm and dry as possible, guard against shock and exposure…and stay away from Frankie Webb.''

''Okay.'' Her response was much fainter than she had intended, revealing that she was disturbed by the presence of the runaway prisoner.

Seth reached out, cupping her cheek, caressing her wind-numbed flesh with his callused thumb.

''Don't worry. Webb would be a fool to try anything. I'll see you safely to Denver. One way or the other.''

For a brief moment, she closed her eyes and surrendered herself to his promise.

Seth would take care of her.

Seth would never leave her.

Then she stiffened as reality washed over her like a chilling wave. Some promises were impossible to keep. Hadn't she already learned that lesson well?

Once before Seth had offered her the same sentiments. When they'd married, he'd been well aware that her background included more than two dozen foster homes and an unsettling childhood with a mother who was diagnosed as being schizophrenic. When Elizabeth had gone to college, she'd vowed that she would never live a life of uncertainty again—and Seth had understood that.

Or so she'd thought.

When she'd met Seth, a colleague had told her that Seth was a professor at NYU. But what she hadn't known was that, just before meeting her, he'd tendered his resignation from the university so that he could accept an offer to be a stunt pilot. Mere days after their whirlwind honeymoon, he'd returned home, dumped a box of belongings on the couch and informed her he'd finished his last day of teaching.

Looking back on that day now, Elizabeth supposed that he'd tried to talk to her. He'd tried to explain how he'd been offered a marvelous opportunity to work with the vintage planes that he loved. He'd carefully underscored the historic importance of his work.

But Elizabeth's mind had centered on one thought alone.

A stunt pilot.

He wanted to be a stunt pilot.

The mere thought had filled her with horror. In her opinion, the only thing riskier than earning a living as a pilot was to earn a living as a stunt pilot. What kind of job was that for a man who'd promised her security and serenity?

In the end, she hadn't even given him the opportunity to compromise. His goals for the future terrified her, and she'd refused to live with that fear. But at the time, it had seemed just as unfair to trap Seth into a job he didn't like. If she'd refused to let him fly for a living, he would have grown to resent her.

So she'd left him. She'd waited until he was on his way to yet another air show, packed her belongings and left.

Seth's thumb grazed her chilled lips, and Elizabeth jerked back to the present. She straightened, pulling away, putting more than physical distance between them.

Seth stood and took the flashlight from its nest in the snow. "Stay with him a minute."

"Where are you going?" The words bolted from her lips as if she feared he would never come back and she hated herself for the telling weakness.

"I've got to cover Caldwell with a blanket or something. It's the least I can do."

Elizabeth bit her lip. Surely Seth wasn't blaming himself for the man's demise.

But as she examined his hard jaw, she knew he was.

"You did the best you could," she called after his swiftly retreating figure.

It was the absence of the squeak of snow against his boots that revealed he'd stopped.

"Did I?"

The words were so dark and forbidding, she felt obligated to continue. "We all could have been killed outright. Because of you we're on the ground and breathing—and we'll be all right."

She tried to infuse her statement with as much optimistic certainty as she could muster, but a mocking inner voice taunted her, reminding her that mere words couldn't ensure their survival.

"I hope you're right," Seth said. Then he continued to plow his way through the snow…leaving Elizabeth to wish that there was something she could do or say to ease his torment.

Seth approached the FBI agent's body with as much care as he could before necessity demanded that he flip on the flashlight in order to traverse the last few yards.

Dead. One of his passengers was dead.

Guilt coated Seth's tongue and choked his breathing. If he'd seen the cliff sooner, he could have altered the glide path of the plane, steered clear and prevented the man's massive injuries.

Damn, why hadn't he reacted a split second faster?

His throat grew tight, and Seth swiped at a blanket he'd seen earlier. The wind would have tugged the woolen square away except that the binding had snagged on a jagged piece of metal.

Pushing his emotions into the deep, dark corners of his mind, Seth forced himself to close the last few feet. Then he crouched beside the dead man.

Wriggling his fingers into his pocket, he removed a small jackknife and cut through the man's tangled seat belt. After laying the blanket in the snow, he dragged the body into place and wrapped it in the woolen shroud.

Seth was about to tuck the last corner around Caldwell's face when the light caught the rivulets of blood at the man's temple and highlighted the extent of the damage.

As well as something more...

Reaching for the flashlight, Seth aimed it more directly on Caldwell's injuries. Kowalski had said that Caldwell had been conscious and coherent after the impact, but judging by the massive injuries Seth saw, he didn't know how such a thing could be possible.

"What the hell..." he rasped when the golden beam highlighted a small, black-rimmed hole above the agent's right ear.

The cold seeped into his bones as Seth absorbed the significance of what he saw. Caldwell hadn't died of injuries sustained in the crash. He'd been shot. Execution style.

Suddenly, the cold was biting, the wind intense. Remembering that he'd come to retrieve the agent's pistol, Seth reached beneath the blanket. His heart thudded in his ears when he realized the weapon was gone.

Adrenaline pumped through his body with renewed force. Diving toward the flashlight, he hit the off button, then panted in the darkness. When Seth had conned Nealy into believing that Frankie Webb was armed, he'd never dreamed that his words might prove prophetic. Stan had said that Webb had attacked him and stolen the cuff keys. Frankie must have gone to Caldwell next, stolen his gun and shot him in cold blood. The confusion of the fire must have masked the discharge.

Lizzie.

He had to get her out of the open and into the shelter of the plane. He had to get them all out of the open.

Fastening the blanket as securely around Caldwell as he could, Seth grabbed the flashlight and ran back in the direction he'd come. Suddenly, the stakes of survival had become much more complex. Again and again, Seth was reminded of the convict's reactions in the terminal when the FBI agents had attempted to restrain him. Frankie's words echoed in Seth's ears.

"You'll both pay for that. If I have to hunt you, and your families, and your friends until the day you die, you'll pay."

Had Frankie taken the opportunity to exact his revenge? Would he continue killing? In his twisted frame of mind, would he delight in torturing the survivors of Flight 356?

Swearing, Seth realized that they all had to be on their guard. Not only did they have the cold and weather to fight, they had to disarm and contain Frankie Webb as well.

As Seth neared the spot where he'd left Elizabeth and the injured FBI agent, he struggled to come to terms with what he'd just seen—as well as the inevitable ramifications.

Killing the FBI agent and taking the man's gun had been a brazen move on Frankie's part. By following the media blitz surrounding the trial, Seth had learned that serial murderers generally killed to release tension and stress. Hell, what could be more stressful than a plane crash?

Added to that, once serial killers felt the rush of the hunt, they tended to repeat their acts again and again with greater frequency until they were finally apprehended. If that were true, then the survivors found themselves in an untenable situation. Suddenly, they'd become possible targets to the convicted murderer.

Granted, they still had the upper hand over Frankie Webb, he reassured himself. They had the shelter of the plane, access to limited supplies, a weapon of their own and the sheer force of numbers. But by killing the FBI agent, Frankie had displayed his need to kill. After what he'd seen, Seth didn't trust Frankie enough to use his common sense and leave them all alone. Not when the cold would eventually drive the convict back to the only available shelter.

Elizabeth looked up as he approached, and Seth directed the flashlight beam in the opposite direction—ostensibly to keep from shining the light in her eyes, but actually to keep her from reading the worry he was sure was clearly stamped on his face.

"Come on, we're going back to the plane," Seth said abruptly.

"I thought you wanted to wait until—"

"It's getting colder out here now that the fire's died down. We've got to get back."

He gave Elizabeth the flashlight and ordered her to gather the first-aid supplies.

"How are you going to get Stan to the plane?"

"Carry him."

Crouching, he took the wounded man's arm, prepared to swing him into a fireman's lift. At the disturbance, Stan jerked, coming to consciousness so abruptly that his body bolted into a near-sitting position.

"Easy, now," Seth said, physically restraining the larger man and pinning his arms in place as Stan's body quivered, then relaxed.

Bending low enough for the FBI agent to see his expression, Seth said, "I've got you patched up for now, but I'm going to need your help getting you to shelter. Do you think you can stand?"

Beads of perspiration were gathering on Stan's upper lip and forehead, but he nodded.

"Frankie—"

"He's run into the woods."

Stan grasped Seth's wrist in a viselike grip. "You've got to find him. You've got to bring him back. The man's insane, I tell you. He enjoys kill-ing—*enjoys* it. For him, it's a game of cat and mouse."

The agent hitched a bloody thumb in Elizabeth's direction. "She'll be the most...likely victim, so keep...her close. But even though the rest of us don't...fit his usual profile, there's no telling what the man will...do. He swore that he'd make me...and my partner...pay...if he ever got loose." Stan's eyes glittered with tears. "Don't...let him. Don't let him do...anything more."

The speech sapped Stan of what little strength he had. He wilted, and his eyes grew hooded with ex-haustion.

Between the pair of them, Seth and Elizabeth man-aged to half-lift, half-pull Stan upright. Then Seth looped the larger man's arm over one shoulder.

"This will hurt like hell, Stan, but you've got to stay with me, okay?"

Elizabeth bit her lip as Stan cried out in pain. The man struggled to help, but even so, Seth was forced to nearly drag the FBI agent to the shelter.

Halfway to their destination, they caught the at-tention of the other passengers. Ricky gripped Mi-chael Nealy's arm and tugged the man forward.

"Come on. Let's give them a hand."

The two men ran to greet them. From that point,

they carried Stan to the opening, then hefted him inside.

Elizabeth, who had been following with the flashlight and first-aid kit, was the last to arrive. She stood shivering next to the wreckage, too tired to haul herself into the shelter. Since Seth was busy with Kowalski, she leaned against the mound of snow caused by the skidding plane. Mere hours earlier, time had seemed to race past her. Now, the ticking minutes stretched into oblivion, creeping snaillike toward a possible rescue.

Already, the cold was numbing. Her body ached with a ferocity that made clear thinking nearly impossible—and the bump on the head she'd received was far less severe than the injuries sustained by Stan Kowalski or Peter Walsh.

Peter.

She clung to the name, to the sense of purpose that came with it. Before being sent away from the wreckage near the wing, he'd been cradling his arm. Someone had to see to him.

"Miss? The pilot sent me to get you and tell you to get inside the plane."

She looked up to find Ricky studying her. He extended a huge paw covered in fur-lined mittens.

Liz fought the urge to sigh in envy. What she wouldn't have done for an hour in those mittens. A minute.

Taking the proffered hand, she allowed herself to be hauled into the shelter—only then realizing how cramped the small space was going to be with so many occupants.

It took all her effort to force her brain to string her thoughts into some coherent pattern. Finally, she asked, "Did Mr. Walsh make it inside?"

"Over here."

Following the sound of the man's voice, Elizabeth felt her way into the darkness of the fuselage until she found Peter Walsh huddled in the rear corner seat that she had so recently vacated.

"I'll look at your arm, if you like."

The man was ashen. Perspiration covered his face and had given his features a greasy sheen.

As a child, Elizabeth had spent most of her summers at state-run camps for foster children. Relying on the limited first-aid knowledge she'd gleaned from the seminars, Elizabeth ordered Walsh to lie in the aisle and prop his legs on the seat—a feat that was nearly impossible with the rest of the survivors clamoring for space.

Whipping a blanket from the aisle, she wrapped it around his body as tightly as she could, then bent to examine his arm.

"Broken?"

She started at the low query, but her reaction was nothing compared to the jump of her heart when Seth laid a hand on her shoulder and squeezed.

"I—I can't tell. He seems to have limited use of his fingers, but he can wiggle them. I can't feel anything broken and most of the pain radiates from his shoulder. I think the joint has been pulled out of the socket."

Seth bent to examine the area, "I'd say you're right." He waved his hand in front of the man's face to capture Walsh's attention. Walsh regarded him blearily, his eyes hazed with pain.

"I'm going to reset your arm. It'll hurt like hell, but once I get it back in the socket, it should start feeling better."

Walsh bit his lip, squeezing his eyes closed as Seth took the man's wrist in two hands, then braced his foot on Walsh's side.

"Hold him down as much as you can, Liz."

She nodded and half lay over the man's torso.

"Ready?"

Walsh nodded.

"On the count of three. One…two…"

Without bothering to offer the next count, Seth jerked Walsh's arm, pulling it outward, then allowing the bone to snap back into the socket.

Walsh screamed, his back arching so wildly that Liz was nearly thrown into the seat behind her. Somehow, she managed to keep her grip until the man wilted onto the floor again. He breathed heavily, but it was obvious that the worst of the pain had passed.

Digging into her bag, she retrieved a container of aspirin and the half-filled bottle of Evian water. "Take these," she said after shaking three pills into her palm.

Walsh offered her a weak smile. "Thanks."

''My pleasure.''

She squeezed Walsh's uninjured hand while Seth took a strip of gauze from the first-aid kit and fashioned it into a makeshift sling.

''Don't you think you should be passing that aspirin around to everyone?''

Elizabeth stiffened at the impatient demand. So far, she'd had only a brushing acquaintance with Ernst Gallegher, yet, she was already developing an intense dislike for the man.

When she would have replied, Seth touched her shoulder. ''There are plenty of painkillers in the first-aid kit. Save your supply for now.''

Gallegher's lips thinned, but he didn't argue.

Needing something to keep her brain occupied, Liz reluctantly regarded the food and mini-bottles given to her by Ricky. ''What about the rest of this? Won't we need the foodstuffs and the alcohol?''

''Whatever you do, stay away from the alcohol. It will speed up hypothermia. As for the rest, gather together what you have.'' Seth spoke up, directing the words to everyone present. ''We need to take stock of any food, medications, clothing and anything else that could prove useful. Empty your pockets and your bags—''

''M-mine's still outside,'' Nealy stammered.

''I only want to see what you've got right here, right now. Don't worry about any luggage that's outside or in the underbelly of the plane. The weather is getting worse and we need to concentrate our efforts on basic survival. We'll take stock of the rest of our stuff tomorrow when it's light.''

He took the strap to Liz's bag. "Put whatever items you find that could be helpful in Liz's bag.''

A stunned silence echoed in the small confines. On the other passengers' faces, Liz caught the same expression that must be etched on her own.

They had crashed. They had really crashed.

Seth seemed to read the panic that raced through her body. His hands grasped her waist, and he pulled her against him, tucking her next to his side.

Elizabeth knew she should be strong. She should remain aloof and cool. But she needed that human contact. She needed Seth's strength and warmth.

Not caring what the other passengers thought, she melted into his embrace and wrapped her arms fiercely around his waist.

''We're alive.''

The words were spoken into her ear. The caress of Seth's breath sent a shuddering wave of relief through her body. He was vibrant and real. As long as she wasn't alone, she could survive.

Drawing back, she glanced at the other worried faces turned in their direction.

''What do we do now, Wonder Boy?'' Gallegher said bitterly.

Elizabeth's fingers balled into fists. It was obvious that Gallegher felt the crash had resulted through Seth's ineptitude.

Rage bubbled in her chest. How dare he? How dare this man blame the one person responsible for saving them all? If not for Seth's expertise, the plane could have dropped from the sky or slammed into the same cliff that had claimed one of the wings.

Seth must have sensed her rising anger because he squeezed her waist.

"I think you'd better lower your voice a notch or two, Gallegher," Seth said. When the man opened his mouth to argue, Seth nodded in the direction of Willa Hawkes, who sat trembling, her eyes wide. "You're upsetting the lady."

Gallegher's jaw clenched in an obvious bid for calm. Then he muttered, "We can't just sit here and wait. What if there's a city nearby, or a farmhouse! We won't know if we don't look."

The words died when Seth shook his head.

"No. There's nothing. We'd be able to see any source of light for miles."

"Then try to call someone on the radio," Gallegher demanded.

Seth didn't immediately answer. Finally, he raked his hands through the waves of his hair.

"I can't do that."

"Why not?" Gallegher snapped impatiently.

"We lost the radio long before we touched down. The crash landing sent a tree through the front controls making any kind of repair impossible."

"Then let's walk out," Gallegher insisted.

"To where? Without knowing exactly where we are or where we're going, we'd be subjecting ourselves needlessly to the elements." Seth shook his head. "No. Our best bet is to stay with the wreckage so that the search party has the largest possible target to find."

Elizabeth followed his sweeping study. In the dim glow being cast by the embers of the fire outside and the harsh beam of the flashlight, it was easy to see that the floor of the plane was strewn with clothing and luggage. Seat cushions lay haphazardly askew, some of them stained with blood.

"What do we do in the meantime?" Walsh asked, his voice tight with pain.

"We make the wait as comfortable as possible for all of us," Seth responded easily.

He reached into the orange duffel bag and tugged on a pair of leather work gloves, clearly turning his mind to the things that would have to be finished before any of them rested. Without speaking, he made the survivors realize that the sooner they got to work, the better.

"Right now, we need to focus on the preparations that will help us through the night." He gestured to the gaping hole. "We've got to clear out this debris, gather important supplies and toss the rest out to make more room."

Seth threw the orange bag at Nealy. "Inside the duffel bag, you'll find some waterproof tarps. You and Gallegher clear the interior as much as you can, then help me cover the hole with blankets and luggage and whatever you can find to keep the wind out."

"What can I do?" Walsh asked, although it was clear that he was about to drop in his tracks.

"You help Mrs. Hawkes, here," Seth said more gently. "Mrs. Hawkes, I'd like you and Walsh to gather any coats, blankets and pillows you can find. Then I want you to make agent Kowalski as warm and comfortable as possible."

"What about me?" Liz asked. "I think I could find a container to fill with snow. If we set it on the dying embers…"

Seth silenced her with another squeeze of her waist.

"We'll worry about that tomorrow. As soon as we've got the opening covered, we'll need to buddy up to combine body heat and do our best to sleep until morning. Get as much rest as you can, because tomorrow we'll be working even harder."

"At what?" Nealy asked in a voice little louder than a whisper.

"Survival. We'll need a fire for warmth and another larger one that we can use to signal any rescue planes. Then we'll improve our shelter. In the meantime, no one leaves the plane." His voice became hard and implacable. "By that, I mean no one."

"But—"

When Gallegher would have argued, Seth slid him a piercing look, daring him to refuse. "We've got a serial killer loose in the woods. He's cold, angry—" he paused before adding, "—and armed."

Chapter Six

Gasps erupted in the small space and the black night was suddenly fraught with tension.

Seth shot a look at Stan, hoping he would back him up, but the FBI agent was unconscious again.

"Come morning, we'll develop a plan of action concerning Frankie Webb. Right now, it's more important for us to get through the night as comfortably as possible."

He stood and Elizabeth watched him begin to gather airline blankets to hang in front of the opening. To anyone else, he appeared cool, collected and in charge. But Elizabeth sensed a finer thread of caution. Often, she caught him casting glances toward the blackness beyond the plane.

Her heart thudded in her chest.

Stan had said that she would be Webb's most likely victim. Elizabeth fit the prisoner's "tastes." She had dark hair and dark eyes.

Her stomach roiled.

What was she going to do?

IT WAS MORE than an hour later when Elizabeth arched her throbbing back and dared to look around her.

The loose wreckage had been cleared from the plane and the opening had been blocked as much as was possible. Then, the survivors had fashioned beds and "nests" of blankets in an effort to give everyone a place to sleep.

As time had passed, Willa Hawkes had been able to shake off the effects of shock, coming to help the rest of "the gang" as she called the motley group. Now, she stood near the door of the plane, clutching her coat lapels tightly around her chin.

Closing the distance between them, Elizabeth slid her arm around the woman's waist and offered her a quick squeeze.

"Why don't you go inside and rest?" she suggested gently.

Willa took a deep breath. "I'm not real...fond of confined spaces."

"Ahh."

The woman's lips twisted in a grimacing smile. "Before I married, I wouldn't have dared to board a plane. But my husband, Ken, loved to travel and he wouldn't dream of leaving me behind."

Willa looked at Elizabeth as if she expected the younger woman to be bored, but Elizabeth motioned for her to continue.

"He was a teacher. That's how we met. I was a spinster librarian in an elementary school who'd long since given up any notions of romance, and he was a tall, dashing newcomer with a passion for history. Every summer we would pack our bags and head off to some exotic locale.'' Her shoulders lifted then dropped. ''I thought that the trip to Denver would be good for me.''

''How did your husband die?'' Elizabeth asked gently, wanting to keep Willa from remembering the crash.

''Cancer. We had a good life together—not everyone gets that, you know. But I miss him.''

Nodding, Elizabeth squeezed Willa's waist again to show she understood.

''Now your young man,'' Willa began.

Elizabeth cut her off before she could continue. ''He's not *my* young man. He's my ex-husband.''

''Mmm.'' Willa's eyes narrowed consideringly. ''You might want to rethink that decision. There's chemistry between the two of you.''

Elizabeth opened her mouth to argue, but Willa seemed suddenly frail and weary.

''I think I'll go inside now,'' she whispered.

Feeling protective, Elizabeth helped the older woman climb into the shelter they'd all created. She hovered by Willa's side until the woman had settled into a seat and covered herself with loose clothing. Then, after Walsh and Kowalski had been laid out as close to a reclining position as possible, the rest of the passengers settled in for the night.

Seth had chosen a spot next to the tarps and blankets—and although the temperature was considerably colder there, Elizabeth automatically joined him.

As she sank to the floor, his arm slipped around her waist and he drew her tightly against him. She sighed when the heat of his body seeped into her own.

Judging by a quick glance at her watch, the evening was still early by her usual standards, but she felt as if midnight had come and gone. She was so tired. So incredibly, achingly tired.

Seth settled his chin on her hair—and if she didn't know better, she would have thought that his lips brushed the top of her head.

"How are you feeling?" he murmured.

"I'm okay."

But even to herself, her statement lacked conviction.

For several long minutes, no one spoke. Then, bit by bit, the silence grew uncomfortable and curiously charged.

Seth was the first to react, lifting his head and drawing Elizabeth's attention to the rest of the survivors.

Do I look like that? she wondered. *Battered, beaten, dazed, confused?*

Self-consciously, she touched a hand to her hair. The tresses had long since fallen from their pins and hung in a tangled mass around her shoulders. Her skin felt gritty and cold and dirty. What she wouldn't have given at that moment for a deep tub filled with hot water and bubbles, room service and a plump bed waiting in the wings. But then, she supposed that they would all have given a king's ransom to be anywhere other than this forsaken mountaintop.

"What happens now?"

The gruff question came from Stan Kowalski. He continued to drift in and out of consciousness. If anything, the binding of the wound in his thigh hadn't helped his condition much. The bleeding might have stopped, but his features appeared more sunken than ever. Despite the blankets and loose clothing piled onto his large frame, he clutched his arms around his body as if wracked with chills. Periodically, his body would convulse in spasms.

They all turned to Seth for guidance, and Elizabeth wanted to shout at them for the unfairness of it all. Seth hadn't planned for this predicament. He certainly wasn't prepared with a checklist of tasks. Moreover, the lot of them should be thanking him for bringing the plane down at all, not regarding him as if he were some sort of enemy who had foisted this scenario upon them.

"There's not much we can do until morning, even if the storm clears. We have limited battery power on the flashlight and it will have to be rationed."

As if to underscore the statement, he extinguished their only source of light and plunged them into darkness.

Soft gasps and cries accompanied the action. Within seconds, there was the rasp of a lighter and a tiny flame appeared to illuminate the blackness.

Automatically, all eyes focused on Michael Nealy and the cigarette lighter he held over his head.

Shifting uncomfortably, he said quickly, "We've got to talk. We can't talk in the dark."

No one argued. That tiny glow was their anchor to reality, Elizabeth realized. Without it, it would be far too easy to believe that the past few hours had been nothing more than a horrible nightmare.

"How long before help can arrive?" Gallegher asked stiffly.

Even though she'd already asked the same question, Elizabeth listened intently to Seth's answer.

"There's an emergency beacon in the tail section of the plane—but with the damage we've sustained and the lack of light, I won't be able to get to it until morning. It could be functioning even as we speak."

"Or it could be bashed to bits like the radio," Gallegher muttered bitterly.

Seth threw the man a quelling look. "In any event, we'll be missed soon enough—"

"When we dropped off the radar, right?" Nealy prompted.

Seth shook his head. "Because of the storm, it might be assumed that we changed our altitude due to the weather. We can't pin our hopes on that. A real concern won't develop until we miss our scheduled arrival." He glanced down at his watch. "We have forty minutes until that time, at least another thirty before it's obvious that we weren't merely delayed." His eyes sparkled in the dark. "But I've got to be honest. The authorities won't be sending any kind of a rescue party until the weather clears."

No one moved. No one breathed.

Seeking some way to alleviate the awful stillness, Elizabeth grabbed her purse and shifted out of Seth's arms. ''Maybe we should check our supplies.''

Seth cast her a look rife with approval. For a brief instant a warmth flared through her body. One that brought with it memories of mornings spent lingering in this man's arms.

Reminding herself that the pressure of the situation was weakening her resolve to resist Seth Brody, she avoided his gaze.

Get a grip on yourself, Elizabeth, she silently chided. *The man hasn't changed these past few years. You can't afford to let your emotions run amok.*

Unwillingly, she remembered the way Webb had winked at her when he'd left the airport waiting room, and she grew colder still.

''Let's look at the emergency supplies first.''

Turning the large, orange duffel bag upside down, Seth dumped the contents onto the floor between his legs. They all leaned over to peer at the jumbled pile.

''We have three boxes of tea, one bottle of vitamins, six candles, a tin of strawberry jam, three cans condensed milk, a can opener, aspirin, a dozen chocolate bars, waterproof matches, a pocket knife, plastic utensils, a whistle—'' He lifted the shiny object to his mouth, filling the cramped fuselage with its shrill sound.

''It works,'' Nealy commented needlessly.

''There's also a mirror, six thermal blankets, a spool of filament thread, a box of fishhooks, tissues, several cans of pork and beans, freeze-dried rations, three Sterno heaters, a rope and...three flares.''

He handed Elizabeth one of the thermal blankets, then tossed the rest to Michael Nealy. ''One for Walsh and Kowalski, then divide the rest.''

Seth waited until they'd grouped together and huddled beneath the scant covering before turning his attention to Elizabeth's purse.

Nealy quickly counted the contents and reported, ''Thirty-six mini-bottles—assorted varieties. Eighteen bags of peanuts, thirteen bags of cookies, six candy bars, five packages of imported cheese, two packages of crackers, and twelve packs of trail mix.''

Walsh offered a low whistle. ''Well, we won't starve anyway.''

Elizabeth grinned. ''With Ricky's samples, we'll be able to live high on the hog for some time.''

''How long?'' Willa asked.

The question shuddered expectantly through the cramped space.

All eyes turned in Seth's direction, even though he couldn't possibly know the answer.

''As long as it takes,'' he offered soberly. ''In the meantime, I'll be in charge of rationing our supplies. Two meals a day, about three to five hundred calories each.''

The group moaned. Then, bit by bit, they settled back in their own prospective nests, leaving Seth and Elizabeth relatively alone.

''A rescue party will come, won't they?'' she whispered.

Seth offered her his best cocky grin. "Hey, don't get all frantic on me, okay? We're going to be fine. Just wait and see." His hand pushed back the hair on her forehead, gently tracing the bump.

"Any updates on the head?"

"It's fine." She didn't bother to elaborate on the pounding pressure that still beat a tattoo against her skull.

"No dizziness?"

"No."

"No nausea?"

"No."

"Good." His eyes warmly traced her features as if he could read them to assure himself of the truthfulness of her answers.

"Aspirin?"

She glanced nervously at the other passengers with their myriad bumps and bruises. "Shouldn't we ration those too?"

Seth held up the bottle, shaking it like a maraca. "There's a thousand tablets in my supply, at least two dozen in yours. I think we're fairly safe in indulging ourselves."

He shook two pills into her hand, then asked to the passengers at large, "Anyone else?"

When all of the survivors raised their hands, he tossed the bottle to Nealy. "Pass them around."

Leaning back, Seth settled onto the pile of cushions and clothing that formed a narrow bed. "Come on. Settle back."

The fact that she'd once been married to this man

didn't seem to matter. Liz was overtly conscious of each line of his body, each nuance of his frame.

Gingerly, she slid into position, her body draped over his, then allowed him to lay his coat, a layer of clothing from one of the suitcases and, finally, a thermal blanket from the emergency kit over top.

His frame was too long for the limited space, so Seth was forced to maneuver into a half-sitting position with his legs bent at the knee. Drawing her body more intimately in contact with his, he shifted, bumping their hips together as he sought a more comfortable position.

Heat flared within her and she tried to sit up, knowing that sleep would be impossible this close to her ex-husband. But Seth snagged her waist and drew her back into place.

"Where do you think you're going?" he asked, the question a caressing threat.

"I'll sleep in the aisle."

"No. You'll stay right here."

"But."

His lips pressed against her cheek.

"Shh."

"Seth, this isn't a good idea."

His lips moved to nuzzle against the hollow beneath her ear. "I think it's a wonderful idea."

"No, really. I don't think we should allow the stress of the situation to affect our relationship. We aren't married anymore. It's wrong to dredge up the past by—"

"Quiet." His lips moved down the line of her jaw.

When he paused, her head seemed to turn of its own volition.

"Elizabeth?"

"Hmm?"

"I'm not letting you go."

She bit her lip, wondering if he'd intended the double interpretation. Could Seth possibly mean something more than this night? Could he possibly mean that he didn't intend to let her run from him again?

Run?

She hadn't run from this man. She'd left him. And with good cause.

But she'd never bothered to explain herself fully to him.

"Get some sleep," Seth murmured, his lips brushing the top of her head.

The hard pillow of his chest rose and fell beneath her.

A lump of emotion lodged in Liz's throat and she fought the inexplicable urge to cry—for herself, for Brent Caldwell, for the other survivors, for Peter Walsh and Stan Kowalski. And for her marriage.

A marriage that had been doomed to fail before it ever began.

IN THE HOURS that passed, Elizabeth decided that their tiny patch of space near the gaping opening wasn't the warmest spot by any means. The blankets that had been fastened as neatly as possible with electrical and duct tape began to work loose within the first hour and the flimsy tarps and blankets did little to cut the bite of the wind. Soon, the heat generated by Seth's body was not only welcome, but vital.

Elizabeth tried to keep her mind off the cold. She tried counting sheep, slow breathing exercises and creative visualization—all to no avail. She seemed doomed to lie awake and worry.

With each minute that passed, she became more and more sure that something was bothering Seth. But what? What could be worse than their present situation? How could a crash, the cold and a wanted man become even more worrisome?

The only thing that kept her from dismissing the niggling worry completely was that she'd always had good instincts where Seth was concerned. And her intuition was telling her that he was keeping something from them all. He was so still beneath her, so tense—and after all the nights she'd spent sleeping in his arms, she knew he was as wide-awake as she was.

More than anything, Elizabeth wanted to talk. She needed to hear Seth's voice and unearth the cause of his strange mood. But with so many passengers listening, she didn't dare. Whatever was bothering him wasn't something he wished to share with the rest of the survivors, and she had to trust him on that point.

Trust.

It was an odd word for an ex-wife to use in association with her former husband, but Elizabeth didn't balk at the implications. Despite everything that had passed between them, she did trust Seth to know what they needed to do in order to survive.

If only she could have trusted his judgment so implicitly when they'd been married.

Shying away from that thought, Elizabeth concentrated on the utter weariness that flooded her body. After such a horrendous day, she should have dropped off to sleep within seconds, Elizabeth decided. But try as she might, she couldn't drift away. Despite the aspirin she'd taken, her muscles throbbed and her head pounded.

Had it only been a day since this awful situation had begun?

No. Not even a full day.

Squeezing her eyes shut, she kept her breathing slow and shallow and her body limp. More than anything else, she didn't want Seth to know that she was still awake. He didn't need to worry about her, while she…

What did she need?

Her throat tightened and she was overwhelmed by the rush of emotions that swarmed her—fear, loss, panic, pleasure.

Pleasure?

Yes. As much as she might want to deny such a reaction, she couldn't lie to herself about the infinite joy she felt at seeing Seth again.

Over and over, she had tried to ground her emotions in reality. She'd reminded herself that their relationship was finished—at her insistence.

Even so, there was a part of her that felt more alive than it had in years.

Shifting, she tried to avoid the musky scent of his body, the hint of the same woodsy cologne that she had given him once so long ago.

He still wore the same brand of cologne.

Elizabeth stifled an impatient sigh. Her reactions to the situation were juvenile. She was behaving as if this man were the object of some adolescent crush and he'd returned to woo her. Nothing could be further from the truth. Neither of them had bargained on seeing the other.

But she had loved him. Once.

Her brain jerked away from that thought as if it were a yawning chasm.

No. She couldn't allow herself to be sucked into Seth's life. She couldn't live with the uncertainty. She wouldn't *be* the woman she'd been then.

Frowning, she realized that she'd hit upon the crux of her resistance. Three years ago, Elizabeth had been a newly graduated advertising student about to begin her first position with a major corporation. She'd worked hard to get where she was—grad school, internships.

But in all that time, she'd never lived alone. She'd moved from foster care to dormitory living to sharing a multitude of apartments with a multitude of roommates.

Then she'd met Seth.

Looking back, she supposed that her first mistake had been exchanging roommates for a husband without ever having tried her wings first. She'd been so sure that Seth would provide her with everything her life had ever lacked: security, stability, love.

She shuddered when she thought of how naive she'd been. She'd assumed that his life had settled upon a well-ordered track without realizing that he was about to confront crises of his own.

But even as an older, wiser Elizabeth looked back on their brief marriage, she couldn't deny that she was still hurt by Seth's career decisions. Incredibly hurt. Although she and Seth had shared a passion like none she'd experienced before or since, there had been no emotional intimacy between them, no blending of thoughts and goals. She'd had no idea that he'd hated his job at NYU enough to quit—and he'd been unaware how important it was for her to succeed in the top advertising theater of Manhattan.

She'd been stunned when he'd confronted her with a fait accompli. But she'd felt even more betrayed when he'd finally bothered to sit down and talk to her about the changes in his life. He hadn't even listened to her concerns. Instead, he'd been wrapped up in the plans he'd made for them both. He'd been so sure that she'd jump at the chance to quit her own position and move "out West" with him. When she'd dared to voice her misgivings, he'd brushed aside her concerns and insisted she would "love the adventure."

But Elizabeth had never wanted adventure.

She'd wanted a home.

They never should have married, she told herself

again. The two of them should have indulged in a brief affair. Then the ties between them wouldn't have been nearly so painful to sever.

"What's wrong?"

She jerked when Seth spoke next to her ear.

"Wha—"

"You're suddenly tense."

She shook her head, but when Seth refused to back away, she offered, "Leg cramp." She doubted that Seth believed the explanation, but nothing could have forced her to tell him the truth.

Just as she would never admit that she had already spent most of the night thinking of him.

Chapter Seven

When the first hint of color began to lighten the edges of the windows, Elizabeth couldn't remember anything looking so welcome. She must have fallen asleep at some point because when she woke up, she was alone. During the night, Seth had eased from beneath her, retucked the blankets and clothes they'd piled over them for warmth, then slipped out of the plane to the snowy field beyond.

Elizabeth forced herself to count to one hundred, then, just as silently as Seth had done, she stood and crept outside.

Seth stood with his feet planted firmly apart, his hands on his hips, staring at the twisted wreckage. Gusts of frigid wind-whipped snow whirled around his blunt silhouette.

It was a miracle that they were alive, Elizabeth realized anew. In the weak light of morning, the debris was even more shocking and the damage path more raw. If the sliding path of the plane had veered another few feet to the left, the jet would have plowed head-on into a rocky escarpment.

A burst of arctic air swirled around Elizabeth's feet and she watched as Seth shuddered, digging his hands into his pockets and hunching into the turned-up collar of his jacket. He seemed to be staring at the place where Brent Caldwell's body had been left. Thankfully, drifting snow had obscured the agent's body.

Something must have alerted Seth to her presence because he spun in the snow, crouching slightly. He only relaxed when he realized who she was.

"Surely you don't mean to chide me for leaving the plane if you've left it yourself," she offered wryly.

To her surprise, he didn't immediately respond to her weak attempt at humor. Instead, his gaze darted around the area as if he expected Frankie Webb to make his move.

The storm itself had eased, but a hazy cloud cover still kept visibility to a minimum. Elizabeth could barely see the edge of the clearing.

Assuming a bravado she didn't feel, she stuffed her hands in her pockets. "I doubt he's out there, you know."

She prayed that Seth wouldn't know that her courage was feigned. As much as she craved being in the open air and away from snoring and snuffling of the other passengers, she didn't relish having Frankie Webb watching her.

"You do?"

"Mmm." She slowly closed the distance between them, wondering why this man drew her to him even when she swore to herself that she was no longer under his spell. "He would have been forced to find shelter himself. Once there, he'd be a fool to leave it so soon."

"And you don't think he's a fool?"

"No. I think he's a psychopath, but from what I've read in the papers, he's by no means a fool."

Which made Webb even more dangerous. His previous murders had been cruelly planned and executed.

"Even so, I wouldn't want you to risk your safety on the basis of a hunch."

She shrugged, reluctantly admitting, "I needed to get out of there, to stand up and stretch. I don't handle crowds too well."

Seth didn't argue, so she supposed he understood—or maybe he remembered. She'd never been overly social. She didn't crave a wild nightlife, nor had she ever done a lot of entertaining. Sometimes, she found it ironic that she'd succeeded as well as she had in the advertising business since she was so opposed to "schmoozing."

She gestured to the plastic bucket at his feet. Judging by the gaily-patterned design on the side, it had once held some sort of Christmas treat.

"Sneaking food out of the airplane?"

He smiled and shook his head. "A long time ago it held caramel corn from a company Christmas party. I brought it out here in the hopes I could siphon some fuel from the undamaged wing. It was one of the containers I managed to gather in the hopes of collecting enough fuel to light a signal fire when we need one.''

She warmed to the use of the word ''when'' rather than ''if.''

''What will you use as a siphon?''

She huddled deeper into her wool coat, glad that she'd brought the knee-length cover-up on her trip to Utah—especially when she noted the way Seth's gaze swept over the garment. For once, she was glad that the robelike design couldn't completely hide the womanly curves beneath.

''When I checked, the fuel tank was leaking. I don't know how much we've already lost through the night, but I managed to rig things so it would drip into a bucket. I doubt there's much left, so I'll keep an eye on things until the tank is completely drained.''

She nodded, finally reaching him and coming to a stop. Turning, she studied the wreckage. The battered aircraft huddled like a wounded bird in the deep drifts, its tender flesh mutilated and twisted.

When she turned again, she caught Seth squinting at the sight, a muscle working in his jaw.

''What went wrong?'' she asked. ''Why did we crash?''

He shrugged fatalistically. ''I don't know exactly. The FAA will examine the wreckage, I'm sure.'' His answer was tight and she wondered if he was still blaming himself for the accident. His hands had balled into fists that pushed against the lining of his pockets. "All I can say is that we lost hydraulic power just before crash landing."

"Do you know why?"

He shook his head. "As far as I can gather, the on-board weather radar malfunctioned. We flew into a microburst without warning." Again, he studied the crippled plane. "We were lucky. In any other circumstances, we could have stalled or lost a wing." His grimace was wry as he gestured toward their landing place. "We were able to touch down before the rocks took care of that little detail."

"Will you lose your business over this?"

He stared at her blankly.

"Won't the loss of your plane shut you down?"

His slow smile was unnerving.

"You really don't know, do you?" he asked.

"What do you mean?"

He gestured to the crippled aircraft. "This is only one plane in a fleet of two dozen."

Her eyes widened in shock.

"Insurance will cover its replacement."

Her thoughts whirled as she tried to assimilate the magnitude of what he was telling her.

"Then you've done well over the past three years."

"Very well."

She licked her lips, realizing that she'd been short-sighted in thinking that Seth would stagnate without her. Somehow, she'd always pictured him unhappy, struggling.

Pining for me.

"I'm glad," she said, but her voice lacked the conviction she'd meant to convey.

"What about you, Lizzie?"

Lizzie. He knew how much she'd detested the nickname, but he'd always persisted in using it.

"I was made associate vice president of the firm."

"Which means you're second in command?"

She shifted uncomfortably, knowing the title she held was somewhat deceptive. "More like fifth or sixth."

"Still, that's something to brag about."

"I suppose." The response was not offered coyly. Instead, she thought hard about all she'd accomplished.

In three years, she'd succeeded beyond her wildest dreams—and she was still on the fast track for promotion.

So when had such milestones ceased to matter? Was it the moment her charter flight crashed on an isolated mountaintop? Or had her dissatisfaction come much earlier?

"Is something wrong?"

She tore herself from her own introspection to regard the man who stood tall and broad in the hazy half-light of morning.

The quiet spooled between them, fraught with the tension of the situation—and more. There was an inherent sexual awareness thrumming in the air that could not be denied.

This time, it was Seth who took a step toward her.

"You've got quite a shiner there." He spoke lowly, clearing his throat to ease it of the sensual tightness.

"Think so?"

She flinched as he probed the area on her forehead and around her eye with a finger. She hissed when he hit a particularly sensitive spot.

"Any pain beside the headache?"

She shook her head.

"Do you feel dizzy? Nauseated?"

His question caused a frisson of alarm. "No. Why do you keep asking me that?"

He shook his head. One of his fingers lingered against the injured area.

"It's possible that you may have a slight concussion. I would have awakened you every hour or so last night if I hadn't been so sure that you weren't sleeping any better than I was." His smile was lopsided and slightly sad. "We will be rescued, Liz."

Her hand raised to clamp around his wrist, but she didn't speak. Despite the wave of apprehension, she couldn't, wouldn't voice her fears. She already knew that it could be days before help arrived. She was well aware of the dangers they faced—cold, exposure, hunger, thirst—as well as the added threat of a serial killer on the loose. She could not—would not—acknowledge that she and Seth were also subject to the emotional turmoil of meeting each other again under such traumatic circumstances.

"I don't suppose you dabbled in medicine since I saw you last," she said at last—as much to break the silence as to garner information of his activities the past few years.

His eyes creased.

"No. Sorry."

She shrugged. "Just my luck."

"I do have some first-aid training."

"Oh?"

"But it's limited. About all I could say for sure was that you don't seem to be in shock, and you certainly don't look like you're drowning."

Laughing softly, she forced herself to push him away.

Don't let yourself get involved with this man again. Don't make the same mistake twice.

"You certainly managed to take care of Stan last night."

His features clouded. "Not well enough. His color is horrible—and the trouble he's having breathing worries me. I'm afraid he's more seriously injured than he's letting on, but I'm not experienced enough to say what."

"Maybe the loss of blood..."

"Maybe."

Again, the silence stretched tautly between them, rife with so many unspoken questions and accusations. More than at any other point since meeting Seth again, Elizabeth became conscious that she was the one who had left him.

"We'd better go join the others," she said abruptly, although there was nothing she dreaded more than spending more time in the plane.

But when Seth didn't move, she couldn't bring herself to take the first step.

"You really should put something on that gash," she finally said.

The cut over Seth's eye was still crusted with blood—some of it fresh as if the wound still bothered him.

Since most of the bandages and gauze pads from the emergency kit had already been put to use, she glanced down at the expensive silk blouse she wore beneath her coat. "I could rip up part of my shirt."

At long last, the corner of his mouth lifted in a crooked smile. "No need. Come with me."

He led her over the familiar field of wreckage to the nose section of the plane.

They were only a few yards away when Seth suddenly squinted at a shadow moving in the trees and grabbed her arm. Swearing, he threw her to the ground just when a shot exploded in the silence.

"Get down and stay down, or I swear I'll shoot you both here and now."

Liz covered her head with her arms, recognizing Frankie Webb's voice and sure that he wouldn't hesitate to kill them. But within seconds, she heard the man jump into the snow and run in the direction of the trees beyond.

Seconds later, the woods echoed with his mocking laughter. "Fools, fools! Do you think I'll let any of you off so easily?"

Seth shifted and shouted, "Turn yourself in, Frankie. You can't live out here. Not without proper supplies. Your grievances are with the law, not us. Come on back, and we'll talk things over."

"You really are an idiot, aren't you? Just like that stupid FBI agent. He thought I was so shaken up by the crash that I wouldn't try anything. But he was wrong."

"Which FBI agent are you talking about, Frankie? The one you attacked? Or the one you killed?"

There was no answer. For long seconds, Seth held Elizabeth in the snow, his body covering her own. Then, he finally took a deep breath and rolled away.

"Are you all right?" he asked, his eyes still scanning the shadows of the forest.

She nodded. "He was there all along? Watching us?"

The thought caused a wave of fear to course down her spine. She and Seth had been standing in the open for at least a quarter of an hour—and all that time Frankie had been watching them. Waiting.

Her body began to tremble in reaction and Seth drew her close.

"Hey, hey," he said soothingly. "He didn't hurt us, okay? He just wanted to scare us into letting him escape."

Looking at the trees again, he took her hand. "Come on. We've got to get behind some cover."

Before she could argue, he pulled her upright and ran to the nose section of the plane.

The last thing Liz wanted was to take shelter in the same place Webb had so recently vacated, but Seth gave her no choice. Once inside, he forcibly pushed her onto the edge of the copilot's seat, carefully avoiding the splintered branch which had pierced the windshield.

She sat shaking, her blood pounding through her veins in delayed reaction.

They could have been killed.

Just like Brent Caldwell.

Elizabeth's mouth parted and she took quick gasping breaths as the full meaning of Seth's shouts shuddered through her system.

Which FBI agent are you talking about, Frankie? The one you attacked? Or the one you killed?

But Webb hadn't killed that man. He'd died from serious injuries caused by the crash.

Hadn't he?

She jumped when Seth framed her face in his hands. "Webb didn't hurt us, Elizabeth."

Hearing the rustling of his jeans next to her, she looked up, only to find that he'd leaned closer. One of his fingers moved to probe the swollen area on her head, but she flinched away from his touch.

"How does it—"

"It hurts!" she cried out, pushing him away. As soon as she did, she regretted it. A catching sob escaped her lips to shiver in the air between them. More softly, she said, "How do you think I feel? I survived a plane crash, remember? Since then, I've been jostled, crowded and bumped—and now I've been shot at by a convicted serial killer."

Closing her eyes, she covered her face with her

hands, afraid of the vulnerability that raced through her. She couldn't let him see her fear. She wouldn't!

Suddenly, strong hands clasped her shoulders, pulling her toward a rock-hard chest. Needing his warmth, Elizabeth circled her arms around his neck. Her fingers dug into the back of his jacket, clutching him as if he were her salvation. Pulling him even tighter against her, she tried to meld her own weak flesh into the strength he exuded so effortlessly.

"I'm sorry. I'm so sorry," she whispered into his neck. "I shouldn't have snapped at you that way. It's just so frustrating...."

He pulled his head back so that he could see her expression.

"Elizabeth, I—"

Suddenly, he stopped. His eyes zeroed in on the trembling curve of her mouth.

Elizabeth shuddered as she read the emotions flashing across his face. Her fingers skidded across the leather of his jacket. Her heart began to pound in her ears, drowning out the sound of his raspy breathing.

"Seth?"

He didn't answer. He leaned closer toward her.

Her eyes quickly traced the arcing curve of his lips before they jumped up to absorb the smoldering blue fire of his eyes. Strong, blunt fingers tunneled into the wild disorder of her hair. Broad palms cupped the back of her skull, firmly drawing her that last fraction that separated them.

A low moan rent the air between them. Elizabeth

couldn't be sure if the sound had come from her mouth or his. All she knew for certain was that their breaths were tangling warmly between them. Their gazes were dueling lovingly.

A quick sigh of delight escaped her throat as their lips met. Tipping her head to the side, she sought the taste and texture of his mouth. His own caress was gentle, hungry, insistent as he moved against her, teasing and exploring her with maddening pressure.

She threaded her fingers through the short, silky waves at his nape, seeking to prolong the tormenting pressure.

A slight tug of her hair forced her to draw back a fraction of an inch. Her eyelids felt heavy and drugged as she opened them. Their gazes clung in surprise and awareness. Elizabeth studied the fierce desire blatant in his expression and wondered if her own features wore the same hungry expression.

"Seth?"

"Shhh…" His arms tightened, crushing her against the hard planes of his chest. One hand moved restlessly up and down her spine. The callused texture of his fingers caused a shivering friction to pass through the layers of her clothing.

"But—"

"Shh, don't talk."

The heat of his gaze scalded her as his head dipped toward hers. He gently brushed his mouth against her cheek, the line of her jaw, the corner of her mouth.

When he lifted his head again, their eyes met in a single, convulsive movement. Desire pulsed between them in a tangible rhythm. Then it was she who pulled him closer, her mouth hungrily covering his.

The moment their lips met, a rush of sensation shuddered through her veins. She eased even closer to him, her hips pressing into the hard muscles of his thighs, her hands sliding down the smooth leather of his jacket, then struggling to reach the bare flesh beneath.

She'd never experienced a touch like Seth's. He had only to look at her to awaken her passion. She'd missed him. Dear heaven, how she'd missed him.

Her hands hesitantly slipped beneath the edge of his jacket. But as her cold fingertips clutched the fabric of his shirt, he drew back.

"We've got to stop. We can't do this," he whispered. "Not here. Not like this."

Not here.

Not now.

Then when?

She bit her lip, squeezing her eyes closed.

His rejection hurt more than she ever would have thought possible.

But what did you expect after the way you treated him?

But when Elizabeth would have continued her inner castigations, Seth tipped her chin up. His lips lightly touched hers, the gesture so sweet, tears sprang to her eyes.

"Don't read my words the wrong way, Lizzie," he whispered. "I want you. I want you more than life itself at this moment." He shook his head as if to clear it of the lingering wisps of abandonment. ''But I won't make love to you when Webb might be waiting and watching.''

The reminder hit her like a cool douse of water.

They were still in danger.

Incredible danger.

Chapter Eight

Blinking, Elizabeth put some distance between herself and Seth, and forced herself to ignore the hunger that thrummed between them.

Don't think about that now. Don't think about Seth. Don't think about Webb.

Clearing her throat, she moved farther away, back to her own seat, then schooled her features into a businesslike mask. Inwardly, she scrambled for something—anything—that would help her gather some control.

"I was going to patch up your eye," Elizabeth blurted suddenly. She congratulated herself when her voice emerged with only a faint trace of the wild abandonment she'd so recently experienced.

"Elizabeth, we—"

She held up a hand to keep him from saying any more.

"No. Please, Seth," she whispered. "I can't take any more. I really can't." She bit her lip when the words emerged much too small and choked with emotions she would rather not name. "I intended to patch you up. Let me do it."

Feeling beneath the cushions of the pilot's seat, he withdrew another, smaller first-aid kit.

She took a deep breath, trying again to be cool and pleasant—nothing more, nothing less. "You're very well prepared."

"I was a Boy Scout."

He flipped the lid open, and fumbled with the contents.

"Here, let me do that," she said.

Wedging herself into the small space between their seats, she selected a fresh package of sterilized gauze and a roll of adhesive tape. Then she took a package of antiseptic swabs, tearing it open and removing a moist square.

"This will probably sting," she warned.

As gently as she could, she dabbed at one corner of the gash.

Seth's sharp, indrawn breath hissed between them and she saw the way his fingers dug into his thighs.

"Sorry," she whispered.

"It's fine," he rasped between clenched teeth.

She reached to clasp his hand, then wondered what had possessed her to touch him when she knew that any sort of intimacy between them was dangerous.

In the faint rosy light, she saw him look at her, *felt* him look at her.

"Why did you leave, Liz?"

She tried to snatch her hand free, but he held it tightly, lacing their fingers together.

Elizabeth tore her gaze away and concentrated on the bandage far more intently than was necessary. "I don't think this is the time or the place to discuss our past."

"I think it's the perfect time—as well as the only place we'll be for a while."

The reminder sobered her, and she stared down at their interlocked fingers.

"Let me finish this first," she said, gesturing to the supplies she held.

He released her, reluctantly. As quickly as she could, she cleaned the wound, then wiped away the trails of blood made by his questing fingers. Despite her careful touch, the gash began to bleed again.

Dropping the soiled swab onto the floor, she covered the laceration with a butterfly bandage.

"That should keep you from bleeding to death anyway." She couldn't prevent the way the words were choked and gruff.

"Wait a minute."

When she would have moved back to the copilot's seat, Seth caught her wrist. Retrieving another package of antiseptic swabs, he tore open the package, then tenderly wiped away the traces of blood from her skin.

The gesture was so unexpected, so inherently gentle and caring that she felt tears stinging the backs of her eyes. She bit her lip to keep from sobbing aloud when Seth lifted her fingertips to his lips and kissed them.

"You've been a trooper through all this," he murmured. "You should be a quivering mass of nerves right now—especially considering your fear of small planes."

Elizabeth grew still. Had it only been the previous afternoon that she'd been so worried about becoming airsick? It seemed like a different woman, a different life.

"Why did you leave me, Liz?"

She waited for some understanding, some sign that she wouldn't have to say the words aloud. When nothing greeted her but silence, she was forced to answer him honestly.

"Because I couldn't be the woman you needed. I couldn't spend my days at home waiting for you to die."

"Die? What are you talking about?"

She chose her words carefully. "You were always looking for a bigger adventure, a more dangerous stunt to perform, a smaller plane to fly. The odds weren't exactly stacked in your favor."

"So you thought I had a death wish?"

She shifted uncomfortably. "'Death wish' might be too strong a term, but I did think you were taking unnecessary risks. I tried to push away my fears," she added huskily. "I really did. But after a while, that was all I could think about, all I could—"

Her explanation was cut short by a frantic cry.

"HEY, WHERE ARE you going? Get back here!"

Seth groaned when the shout echoed across the clearing.

Damn it. Seth didn't want to leave just yet. He needed to be *here* with Elizabeth. He needed to get some answers to the questions that had plagued him for three years. But his responsibilities were again clamoring for attention. As much as he might wish to interrogate Elizabeth, he couldn't.

He stared at her for one more aching moment, then swore and headed toward the opening.

"Mrs. Hawkes? Mrs. Hawkes!"

As he moved into the light, Seth recognized Ricky's voice, and grew numb. Willa Hawkes had been acting strangely since the crash. She'd alternated from shock, to confusion, to a weary coherence. What could possibly be wrong now?

Jumping from the nose section, he turned to help Elizabeth, then ran through the snow in the direction of Ricky Brummel. In his arctic coat, the man looked like a roly-poly snowman gone bad.

Seeing them, Ricky waved his arms, then pointed in the direction of the woods.

"She's wandered off. She went that way—the same way that convict escaped yesterday."

Seth grimaced. "That's all we need, someone wandering around in the forest with a murderer on the loose." He pushed aside the questions pummeling his brain. When he noted that Elizabeth was still standing in the open, he frowned. "Get back to the plane with the others."

"No."

Her blunt refusal was so unexpected that he stared

at her, taking in the wide eyes, the pale skin and the latent stubbornness hardening her jaw.

"What do you mean, 'no'?"

"I mean, I'm going with you."

"Elizabeth—"

"You can waste all the time you want arguing, but I'm going with you. Willa is frightened and confused. She admitted to me last night that she's claustrophobic and a night cramped in the plane may have brought back her shock. So far, Ricky and I have been the only people who have managed to calm her."

Seth sighed in frustration, realizing she was right. Then, sensing Elizabeth would probably follow him anyway, he said resignedly, "Fine. Let's go. But stay close to me, damn it."

He forged through the snow, trying to trample a path for Elizabeth as he went. It was easy enough to find Willa Hawkes. She'd barely disappeared into the stand of pines before stopping. She stood dazed, confused, murmuring, "My books. What have they done with my books?"

Seth would have charged up to her and dragged her back to shelter, but Elizabeth touched his arm and motioned for him to remain silent.

"Willa? Willa, do you remember me? We were on the plane together."

Willa blinked at her in obvious surprise.

"Yes, I'm sure you remember," Elizabeth continued. "We've chatted several times. You helped me clean up the plane last night."

Willa stared at her blankly, but Elizabeth pretended not to notice. Wrapping an arm around Willa's shoulders, she drew her irresistibly toward the clearing and the plane. All the while, Seth nervously regarded the shadows.

They hadn't seen anything of Frankie Webb during the incident, but Seth had a feeling that the convict would be making another appearance before the day was through. Frankie had no food, no supplies, no real warm clothing. He would be drawn back to the survivors like a moth to a flame.

Seth didn't relish the complication. With one FBI agent dead and the other severely injured, Seth wasn't at all comfortable with the idea of keeping a serial killer subdued until they could all be rescued.

But what other choice did he have?

A prickling at the nape of his neck added to Seth's sensation of being watched.

"Pick up the pace, Elizabeth," he murmured under his breath.

She glanced questioningly over her shoulder and he said, "I think we've got company in the woods."

They hurried back to the plane, the cold snow whipping against their cheeks and making even that relative shelter seem inviting.

Elizabeth moved to help draw Willa inside, but at the edge, the older woman balked, obviously terrified at returning to the cramped quarters.

"My books," she stated determinedly, apparently finding ample reason to stay outside.

"We'll look for your books when it gets a little

warmer. Right now, you need to get out of the wind.''

Willa's jaw set, then she stumbled and tried to make her way past Seth.

''I've got to find my books.''

Seth wrapped an arm around her waist, forcibly restraining the woman. She was surprisingly strong considering her condition.

''Mrs. Hawkes—''

''No. I won't leave them out here. I can't. They're like children, don't you know?''

''Ms. Hawkes. I really must insist that you—''

''Damn it, he's convulsing!''

They turned en masse to find Ricky scrambling back into the plane.

Gesturing for Elizabeth to precede him, Seth scooped Willa into his arms and deposited her unceremoniously into the shelter, then swung into place himself.

As soon as his eyes had adjusted to the darkness, Seth saw what had alarmed Ricky. Stan Kowalski had rolled from his seat to the floor. His arms and legs flailed wildly, his eyes rolling back in his head.

''What the—''

At the sight of the agent's torment, Willa grew suddenly docile, sinking into a chair and wrapping her arms tightly around her body.

Kowalski began to gag and choke and Seth motioned for Ricky to help flatten the man into the aisle. Even as he was settled into place, Stan's body grew rigid, his chest swelled in a pained breath. Then, the air escaped his lungs with something akin to a sigh and he stared sightlessly up at the ceiling.

"Who knows CPR?" Gallegher shouted.

Elizabeth was the only person to respond. Stepping over Stan's body, she positioned herself between a row of seats and placed her hands on the man's chest. Seth instantly took position near Kowalski's head to apply artificial respiration.

"Ready?" Elizabeth asked.

"On three."

Seth tipped Stan's head back and opened the man's mouth. But as soon as the man's lips parted, blood oozed from between them.

"I need more light here," Seth growled.

Instantly, the flashlight was switched on and aimed into the shadowy recesses.

Willa sobbed when the golden beam illuminated the blood that seeped from Stan's nose and ears.

"God," Michael Nealy whispered from the shadows.

Elizabeth automatically continued to apply pressure to Stan's chest, but Seth reached out to stop her.

"He's gone," he whispered, his throat tight, his chest heavy.

"But—"

"He wouldn't be hemorrhaging like that unless he had massive internal injuries. CPR won't bring him back."

THEY WRAPPED Stan's body in a blanket. Then, with the help of Ricky and Michael Nealy, Seth carried the two deceased agents to a sheltered spot beneath the trees and covered them with a piece of sheet metal to protect them as much as possible from the elements.

Once again, Nealy became frantic about his luggage, wanting to find his coat. When his coat was discovered, he wanted his toiletries, his carry-on bag, his suitcase. Finally, irritated with the man's frantic obsession with his possessions, Seth sent everyone inside the plane for cover.

Although the passengers hurried back to the plane, Seth lingered, his profile limned in hazy light. He looked so grim and unrelenting that Elizabeth knew he was blaming himself for the two deaths.

"You couldn't have done anything more, Seth," she said as she approached.

"I could have prevented the crash."

"How? The weather was to blame."

"I should have delayed the flight, pursued a course around the storm."

"From what you've told the other passengers, you couldn't have predicted the microcells. You did your best to escape them, but by then it was too late."

She was relieved that he didn't try to argue with her reasoning. Even so, she knew her words hadn't managed to placate him completely.

She shivered as Seth studied the leaden sky. For the moment, the wind had died, leaving an eerie silence that was more menacing than reassuring.

"We'll have more snow before nightfall."

"Is that good news or bad?" Liz shoved her hands

into her pockets in an effort to find any patches of warmth that she hadn't already exploited.

He breathed deeply, his gray eyes scanning the rolling drifts. The snow had been bisected by a deep gouging trough caused by the crippled plane touching ground and skidding to a halt.

"The good news is that the snow will keep temperatures warmer."

"And the bad news?"

"The snow will begin to obscure the wreckage and the damage path."

"Making it harder for us to be found."

He nodded.

"So what do we do now?"

Seth planted his hands on his hips and made a slow circle.

"We do the best we can with what we have." His arm made a sweeping gesture. "The plane will serve as a fairly good shelter, but I've got to get to the tail of the plane to ensure the emergency beacon is transmitting. The rudders crumpled and the beacon is housed nearby."

"Then we'd better get to work."

When she would have made her way back to the plane, Seth snagged her elbow. He waited until Ricky had moved out of earshot, then said, "If Willa takes it into her head to wander off again, I don't want you following her alone, all right?"

Her brows rose. "I hadn't planned on taking a stroll around the mountainside."

"No, but I don't want you taking care of...

personal business without an escort. Continue to use the lavatory in the plane like we all did last night.''

Despite the fact that she'd once married this man and had been intimate with him, she felt herself flush.

''But we haven't heard a peep from Webb since this morning. For all we know, he could be miles away. What would be the use of harming us?''

''Frankie Webb is a furious, frustrated man. He kills for pleasure. And he'll do whatever he can to ensure he isn't captured again. I'd bet the farm that the man attempts to take over the plane, maybe even hold us all hostage. By now, he's got to be cold, hungry, and tired. His only hope of survival is to rejoin us, and his only hope of escape is to keep us under his control.''

A chill that had nothing to do with the cold skittered down her spine.

''We have everything he needs—the beacon, the plane and food.'' As if to underscore his point, Seth added, ''From what I've seen and heard about his previous trials, Frankie Webb has no regard whatsoever for the lives of others. If he thinks that getting rid of a few inconvenient passengers might keep him alive and out of the law's clutches, he'll do it.''

Seth checked to ensure that no one was watching them, then slid a tiny derringer from his jacket. He tucked the weapon into her pocket.

''This was Stan's. I found it hidden in an ankle holster. I want you to keep it with you at all times.''

''No, I—''

"You're the only other person I know well enough to trust with a weapon." Her heart warmed until he continued, "Willa Hawkes is in shock, Nealy is too excitable, Walsh isn't looking too well…and Gallegher's a pain in the butt."

So he trusted her by default.

Elizabeth looked down at it blankly, then shook her head and tried to push it into his hand.

"No, really—"

"This isn't a debatable issue, Liz. The gun is loaded, the safety on."

She turned it from side to side, reluctant about keeping it.

"Webb will only get more and more dangerous with each day that passes," Seth insisted. "Of us all, you are the one person most at risk."

She felt the color drain from her face.

She was young and female. She had dark hair, dark eyes and a professional background. All of those traits were Frankie Webb's victims' trademarks.

Lifting the derringer, she closed one eye and tested the sight.

"Do you think you can shoot him if necessary?"

She nodded. "If he's close enough."

Seth smiled in approval, then jerked his chin in the direction of the plane. "Go on and head back."

She took two steps, then turned when she realized Seth didn't mean to follow her.

"Aren't you coming?"

He shook his head. "I'm going to take a look around."

Her brows rose.

"Then I'll go with you," she insisted.

His lips thinned.

"Not this time. I'll be looking for Frankie Webb's trail."

Although the last thing she wanted was to walk into the woods where a convicted serial killer might be hiding, she couldn't help saying, "Don't you think it's unwise to go alone?"

"I won't be long."

"But—"

"Get back to the plane, Elizabeth."

She stiffened at his high-handed tone. It was the same didactic, professorial command that had grated on her nerves when they were married. After all, she wasn't a child or some intellectual lightweight to be told what to do and when to do it.

But when his eyes flashed in warning, she didn't bother to argue. Instead, she did as she'd been told…for the most part.

As soon as a glance over her shoulder confirmed that Seth was out of view, she retraced her steps and hurried after him.

"Don't go off by yourself," she muttered under her breath. "Do as I say, not what I do."

Why hadn't she remembered the way Seth had always wanted to wrap her in cotton wool and place her on a shelf? He'd treated her like some fragile porcelain doll that didn't have a brain in her head.

He'd never acknowledged that her job took a good deal of finesse and even more intelligence. Being a professor of history, he'd simply assumed that she didn't know much of anything other than the latest cat food jingle.

Fanning the fury of past wrongs helped to keep her warm, and she continued her inner tirade for nearly a hundred yards before stopping short and ducking behind a boulder.

Seth had halted at the edge of a small clearing. Brows furrowed, he searched the shadows of the trees, looking for something, anything, to tell him that Frankie Webb was near.

"Frankie?" he called out loud. "Frankie, you'll die out here without the proper food and protection. Come back to the plane, no questions asked."

His only reply was silence.

"Frankie, it's stupid to stay out here in the woods. You'll freeze to death if the animals don't get you first."

No answer.

Elizabeth crouched lower, wondering what had caused Seth to stop here when there seemed to be no more signs of life than there had been earlier on the trail. Perhaps Seth had heard her footsteps crunching through the snow and mistaken them for Webb's.

Without warning, a shape lunged out of the trees. Frankie Webb lifted his pistol, aimed, then swore when the click of an empty chamber told them all that he was out of ammunition.

Before Seth could react, Frankie threw the gun

into the snow, then dived forward, tackling Seth and grappling for control of Seth's pistol.

Elizabeth swore, scrambling from her hiding place.

"Get back! Get back!" she shouted, leveling the derringer at the tangled forms.

But if the men heard her, they gave no sign. Frankie had Seth's wrist with both hands and was slamming it against the ground in an effort to loosen Seth's grip on the weapon.

She had to do something. Quick. If Frankie got hold of another gun...

Lifting her own pistol into the air, she released the safety with a trembling thumb, then shot twice, the recoil causing the second bullet to whiz past Frankie's head.

The convict looked up, swore, then stumbled and ran into the trees.

Seth rolled to his feet, and without so much as a glance in her direction, stormed after Frankie.

Elizabeth scooped up Frankie's abandoned pistol and followed fast on Seth's heels—partly from the need to help, but even more from her need to avoid being alone in the woods. She'd seen the flash of hatred in Webb's bleak eyes, and she'd known that Seth had been correct in assuming that the man would do anything to avoid capture.

Chapter Nine

Gasping, Elizabeth struggled to keep up with the fleeing forms. Barely a hundred feet had passed before she lost sight of Frankie. Within a few yards, she noted that Seth had stopped next to a frozen stream. He was bent at the waist, his hands braced on his knees as he gulped the frigid air into his lungs.

Wheezing from the unaccustomed effort, she stumbled to a stop beside him.

"I don't...know when I got...so out of shape," she gasped.

"Altitude," was his single-word response.

She collapsed onto a fallen log that was only partially covered in snow. Now that the adrenaline was ebbing, she became uncomfortably aware of the trembling of her limbs. Her head swam dizzily, and her stomach churned with a hint of nausea.

"Where...did he go?" she said, still puffing.

Seth slowly straightened. "I don't know. I lost...him a few yards...back. As soon as he hit the ice...I couldn't find his...tracks."

As if suddenly realizing that he wasn't alone, he stabbed a finger in the air.

"I thought I told you...to head back to the plane."

Although her limbs were still the consistency of spaghetti, she forced herself to stand.

"I chose to ignore you." She took a gulp of air, her breathing beginning to return to normal. "It's a good thing I did. If I hadn't followed you, Frankie Webb would have rearmed himself by now—and you'd probably have a bullet through your head."

"That is beside the point." Seth grabbed her elbows and hauled her against him, leaning so close that his face was only inches from hers. "I told you to do something, and I expect you to follow my orders."

"Why? Because I'm not capable of making decisions for myself?"

"I think I'm in a better position to analyze the situation—"

"Because you're a big, bad, Harvard Ph.D., and I'm only a lowly advertising executive?"

"What the hell?"

"You never did acknowledge that I had skills and talents of my own, did you, Seth? I had no interest in history, and flying in your planes made me sick. So you assumed that I wasn't capable of coherent thought. You never bothered to admit to yourself or to me that my analytical skills rivaled your own—even without the formal training. As far as you were concerned, I was barely competent enough to balance the checkbook or organize a shopping list."

She ended in a near shout, her hands lifting to pound on his chest. As the words echoed into oblivion, she gradually became aware of Seth's shocked expression.

"I never thought any of those things, Elizabeth," he said after several long, silence-fraught moments.

"Didn't you?" she responded bitterly, the words husky with remembered anger and frustration.

"No. I thought you were one of the most creative and dynamic people I'd ever met. The things you could do with a pencil and a sketch pad…"

She blinked, staring at him. Bit by bit, she began to realize that he was honestly stunned by her accusations. Even so, she couldn't help pushing her point. "You might have admired my artistic flair, but you didn't think too much of my intelligence."

He shook his head in patent bewilderment. "I thought you were brilliant."

She snorted and he gripped her tighter.

"Damn it, Elizabeth, I used to stand in the doorway of your studio and watch you for hours."

The statement brought a clear picture of Seth with his shoulder propped against the doorjamb, his eyes watching every move she made.

She grimaced. "What you mean to say is that you used to check up on me."

"No. I was fascinated by the way your mind worked—your brain used to leap from idea to idea, embellishing, reaching, stretching, while my own seemed doomed to travel from point A to point B."

His voice was tinged with sadness. "I never thought you were stupid or that you needed to be watched."

"Then why did you send me back to the plane so that you could wander—*alone*—through the woods?"

His hands slipped around her back, drawing her into the circle of his embrace.

"Because I couldn't bear to see you hurt."

"I can take care of myself," she said mutinously.

He studied her with narrowed eyes. "Perhaps." His lips twitched in a grin. "But you can't shoot worth a damn."

She felt the heat stain her cheeks.

"I've never shot a pistol before."

"Really," he drawled mockingly. "So why didn't you tell me that in the first place?"

Not waiting for an answer, he took her wrist and turned her in his embrace until her back rested against his chest. Then, he lifted both her arms.

"Hold the pistol with two hands and sight down the length of the barrel. Squeeze the trigger—don't jerk it. Once the shot is fired, be prepared for the recoil."

She grimaced, remembering the way her second shot had gone wild.

Still holding her wrists, Seth bent to whisper next to her ear. "Aim for that bent pine tree. There's a knot in the trunk. I want you to hit the middle of the knot."

Judging by the poor shooting techniques she'd already displayed, Elizabeth doubted that she would be able to come anywhere close to a real target, but she did as she'd been told—sighting down the barrel and squeezing.

She flinched at the noise of the report, then opened her eyes to see a neat hole mere inches off center.

"I did it," she said with something akin to amazement.

"Of course you did. Just remember to take your time, aim, squeeze the shot—and keep your eyes open."

At his urging, she took one more shot before he reminded her that they needed to save their ammunition.

Nevertheless, the silence between them as they walked back to the plane was only slightly less strained than it had been earlier. Seth was obviously still irritated by her headstrong decision to follow him.

They were only a few feet away from the clearing when Seth spoke again. "I never meant to hurt you, Elizabeth."

Elizabeth gazed at him in surprise. She'd thought that he was still stewing over her disobedience. She certainly hadn't thought that he was digesting anything personal.

Embarrassed, she looked away. If she looked at him, she would lose control.

"I was a rotten husband, I'll admit that. I should have communicated with you more. I should have told you about the career changes I'd made before we married. I never should have assumed that you'd be as thrilled as I was by the opportunities. And once you'd voiced your concerns, I should have been more patient and understanding.''

He touched her cheek. ''But most of my mistakes were made from inexperience—not from spite. And I never, *never* intended to make you a widow. The fact that you worried about my safety never once crossed my mind.''

She bit her lip, the words she'd uttered earlier returning to haunt her.

''Did you really think I wanted to die?''

He stopped and his finger tipped her chin up so that she would look at him.

Tears gripped her throat and pricked her eyelids. ''You took so many chances,'' she said huskily. ''I didn't see how working in those air shows could result in anything but tragedy.''

''I explained how every move was choreographed for utmost safety.''

''No.'' She shook her head. ''We never discussed the inner workings of the air shows. As you've so adeptly pointed out, we rarely talked about anything. What time we had together we spent in bed.''

He grimaced, realizing she was telling the truth. Stuffing her hands in her pockets, she stared toward the clearing.

Then, since there was no more left to be said, Elizabeth began to walk away.

He caught up to her, snagging her by the elbow. When she dared to look at him, she knew that she'd been premature in her assumptions. There was a great deal left to discuss.

But thankfully, when Seth spoke, he merely said, "I've got to get to the transmitter. Can you help?"

Elizabeth would have done anything to give herself a breather from Seth's disturbing presence, but her pride wouldn't allow her to admit him such a thing. Instead, she assumed a neutral expression.

"Sure. What do we need to do?"

"There's an access panel on the tail section of the plane, but I'll need someone to hold tools and help me clear the drifts of snow out of the way. Most of all, I need someone to cover my back so Webb doesn't try anything."

"But he isn't armed any longer."

She took Frankie's gun from her pocket and handed it to Seth.

"That doesn't mean I trust him," Seth said as he slid the weapon into his own jacket pocket. "If you're up to it, I could use another hand. I trust your instincts more than anyone else's."

His choice of words struck her as funny. *I trust your instincts....*

"I'd like to take advantage of the situation and strengthen our position as soon as possible," he added.

"You make it sound like you're expecting a siege."

His eyes became hooded and bleak.

"I am."

IT TOOK MOST of the afternoon to locate the beacon. Their first task was to remove the mound of snow that had formed around the tail—work that was hard and tedious without proper tools. Except for Walsh, the rest of the survivors helped them, but they were forced to use bits of wreckage, plastic drinking cups and their hands to carve away an opening to the access panel.

Through it all, Nealy worked impatiently— obviously eager to turn his attention to unearthing his luggage. Elizabeth was growing tired of his preoccupation with his own comfort. He was worried about *his* clothes, *his* luggage, *his* spare shoes. But what about Willa, who had only a pair of low-heeled pumps to wear? Or Walsh, who had only a thin overcoat? Or even Gallegher, who didn't seem to have any luggage at all.

Elizabeth paused in her efforts and stared at Gallegher. There was something about the man....

He was rude and belligerent and filled with bitterness. But as much as she wanted to hate the man, there was something in his eyes, a watchfulness, a vulnerability...

An abject pain.

Of all the survivors, he seemed the most concerned about Frankie, constantly drilling Seth with impossible questions about the man's whereabouts. If Frankie weren't a convicted killer, Elizabeth might have thought that Gallegher knew the man. There was a certain familiarity about the way he used Frankie's name. Yet there was no love lost in the tone of his voice.

Of all the passengers, Ricky proved to be the most endearing. Although he was concerned about his missing samples case, he didn't dwell on his misfortunes. Instead, he seemed to have taken upon himself the job of group cheerleader. As they toiled away, he recited a host of knock-knock jokes that were so silly and so old that he had everyone smiling. Even Gallegher's lips twitched ever so slightly.

"Elizabeth, I need your help here."

Seth had been able to rescue a small set of tools from the cockpit, and he had finally managed to free the crumpled panel so that he could uncover the controls beneath.

Hissing at the twinging darts of pain shooting through her cold joints, she moved to hold the emergency mirror so that light was reflected inside the panel.

"Nealy's driving me crazy," she said to him under her breath.

"And Gallegher too." Seth briefly glanced up at the tall, gaunt man. "The way he's so obsessed with Frankie, you'd think he was a cop."

A cop. She hadn't thought of that possibility. It would certainly account for Gallegher's obsession with Webb's criminal nature.

Seth bent back to his task, a lock of hair falling over his forehead. As she watched him work, Liz found herself studying Seth with fresh eyes.

He'd changed over the past few years. As he labored over the delicate components, she was able to see that he was more settled, purposeful, calm....

Happy.

His new life obviously suited him. More than hers suited her.

She frowned, wondering what had caused her to entertain such a traitorous thought. She was happy, she insisted silently to herself. She had a wonderful job, a beautiful apartment and friends in high places.

But even as she insisted that she loved her lifestyle, she realized that her inner protestations were forced. Over the past few years, the pace had grown frenetic and her responsibilities overwhelming. Time and time again, she'd insisted that she was happy with the changes. Didn't they mark the rungs she'd scaled on the ladder of success?

A sigh slipped through her lips.

No. Not really.

It had taken landing on a remote mountaintop for her to realize just how tired she was. She was tired of Paul's demands, his unethical practices, the breakneck pace, the unending deadlines. She'd been racing toward burnout without realizing what was happening. If she continued on the same course, she would...

She would what?

Become like Paul?

Or kill what little enthusiasm still remained for the work she did?

Something akin to horror swept through her body. How had she come to this point so oblivious to her own emotions? How had she allowed herself to become so deeply involved in a career that she didn't really like? Had she been so proud, so concerned with what other people thought of her, that she hadn't bothered to be happy?

Why hadn't she had the courage to walk away from things? Why hadn't she drawn a line in the sand and said enough?

Just like Seth.

Her hands trembled as she realized what she was thinking. For years, she had blamed Seth for the demise of their marriage because he'd walked away from a safe and sensible job so that he could play with his "toy" planes. She'd berated him for being irresponsible and irrational.

Yet, at this moment, she realized that she didn't have the courage to follow his example.

Shame swept through her body. She'd been so unfair, so…

Selfish.

Yes, she'd been selfish. She'd thought only of her own wants and needs. After risking enough to marry a man she barely knew, she hadn't been willing to trust his instincts. She'd been so sure that he was undermining the very foundation of their existence. She'd been so bent on making her life safe and secure, she hadn't allowed him any room to be happy.

"I'm sorry, Seth."

She hadn't realized she'd spoken aloud until Seth looked up, his brow creasing.

"What?"

Since the words had already been spoken, she didn't dare take them back. Not when she had treated him so unfairly in the past.

"I'm...sorry that I didn't trust your decision to leave your job."

His brow rose.

Even though she knew her comment had come from left field, she pressed on. "I've only recently realized how unfair I was. I should have known that you would never take such a decision lightly. I should have given you a chance to explain yourself. Then I should have given you a chance to give your ideas a try."

He was staring at her. Hard. His emotions were completely unreadable, and she wished he would give her just a hint of his thoughts.

"What's happened to you, Liz?"

At any other time, she supposed she would have bristled, thinking that he'd meant the comments as an accusation. But after all that had happened, the struggles they'd shared, she knew that he was merely curious.

"I suppose you could say I grew up."

He shook his head. "You were never immature. That was never a problem between us. If anything, I always worried that your experiences with all the foster homes aged you beyond your years."

Elizabeth blinked in surprise. As far as she could recall, she'd glossed over her years in and out of foster homes. She'd certainly never told him any details.

"After you left, I realized that the uncertainty you must have felt as a teenager merely acerbated the tension between us. I should have courted you longer. I should have put more effort into our marriage."

When she tried to shake away his statements, he continued.

"I could have been more understanding—and I certainly could have broached the subject of changing jobs with a little more tact and diplomacy. But I felt so…so…"

"Trapped," she supplied in a mere whisper. More than at any other time in her life, she understood this man.

After a few quiet moments, Seth turned back to the damaged panel. In a few moments, he was able to uncover the delicate electronic machinery beneath.

"Has it been working?"

Seth shook his head.

Liz bit her lip. She'd hoped that the beacon had been transmitting all this time and that help was on its way.

But she couldn't let herself think of that. Not now. She had to keep her wits about her, ignore the cold and the hunger and the disappointment.

Hold on. Just hold on a little longer.

For hours, she stood by Seth's side, holding tools, running for whatever supplies he needed that could be scrounged from the plane or the first-aid kit, but finally, Seth tightened one of the screws and…

A light flickered from the control panel.

"It's working?" Liz breathed.

Seth's grin was the most welcome sight she'd seen all day.

"It's working."

"How long before someone notices?"

"Any time."

"And how long before help arrives?"

His lips twitched in the first honest smile she'd seen. "If the weather holds, we could be out of here by nightfall."

Nightfall.

The word had a wonderful, lyrical flow to it. Like the word home. Bubble bath. Sleep.

Seth watched the play of emotions cross Liz's features. She was obviously tired, shaken, and hungry—and different, so very different. In the short time that he'd been married to her, he couldn't remember seeing her hair out of place, her clothing mussed or her fingernails in anything other than impeccable condition. Yet at this moment, he didn't think that he'd ever seen her looking so good, so desirable. She was approachable. Soft.

Real.

AFTER EATING a meager meal—a package of peanuts and a portion of chocolate each—the survivors gathered around the small fire that Gallegher and Ricky had made a few yards away from the shelter.

"What next, Seth?" Walsh asked.

Seth frowned. Walsh should have been improving with each hour. Instead, the man was pale, his breathing labored, dry, hacking coughs preventing him from saying anything more.

Squinting into the dipping sun, Seth frowned in frustration. Daylight was ebbing so quickly, and there was still so much to do.

The survivors were staring at him expectantly, waiting for his orders, so he said, "We won't have time to gather enough fuel for a proper signal fire, but we've got to get more wood so we can keep this fire burning through the night. We need branches, logs, anything you can find. Collect plants that are as dry as possible. Dead wood is best since the green stuff won't burn as well and will cause too much smoke to be comfortable. We've got less than two hours before it starts growing dark, so you'll want to move quickly. I want everyone to work in teams. No one goes out alone for any reason and you keep your eyes on one another's backs, understand? Webb is unarmed, but that doesn't mean he's not dangerous."

Gallegher sniffed. "What good will it do us to waste our energy gathering wood when the beacon is working and we could be rescued at any minute?"

Seth was growing weary of the man's constant contrariness, but he didn't rise to the open provocation. Instead, he said, "It sure as hell beats freezing to death, Gallegher."

For more than an hour, they slogged back and forth from the plane to the heavy growth of pines that surrounded them, gathering armloads of branches and bringing them back to the clearing before returning for another load. The work was exhausting, tiring and monotonous. Since most of the trees were mature and weathered, Elizabeth, Seth and Ricky had been forced to plow through the high drifts, singling out the younger and disease-ridden trees and those with branches that had been damaged by the heavy snow. After they carried their finds to the main trail, Willa, Walsh, Nealy and Gallegher dragged them back to the plane.

Elizabeth sighed, arching her back. Her hands and shoulders throbbed in pain from reaching overhead to tug on the heavy branches until they broke away from the tree.

Finally, Seth called a halt to the enterprise. "It's getting cold and dark. Let's head back to the shelter."

Willa, Walsh and Gallegher grabbed a blanket laden with branches and dragged it back to the plane. When an armload of dead wood toppled off and skidded down a gentle hill, Nealy sighed.

"I'll pick it up," he said to the others. "You go ahead."

Seth waited for the man. But once Nealy was out of earshot, Seth didn't immediately follow. Instead, he took Elizabeth's hand, encouraging her to linger with him in the silence.

"You look tired," he said, tugging off his gloves and stroking her cheek.

"I'm exhausted."

"Maybe tonight you'll be able to sleep."

"Maybe," she echoed doubtfully.

Seth led her through the woods at a companionable pace, but as always, his eyes swept the shadows around them. "We could take turns sleeping."

She sighed. "That's probably the only way I would ever be able to nod off."

They were just breaking through the cover of the trees when a series of shouts shattered the winter stillness.

Since a knot of passengers had gathered around the tail section of the plane, Seth and Elizabeth ran in that direction. They hadn't even reached the group when Willa turned to them.

"Somebody broke the beacon."

Elizabeth felt Seth stiffen.

"What?"

The onlookers moved away to show that the beacon housing had been irreparably smashed. Electronic components littered the ground for several feet in either direction, and a huge rock had settled into the snow mere inches away.

"What happened?" Seth asked, his tone tight and dangerous.

Gallegher tipped his chin in the air as if Seth had insulted him. "None of us had anything to do with it. We were all gathering branches for a fire like you told us. It wasn't like this when we brought the last load."

"It must have been Frankie," Elizabeth said, squeezing Seth's hand. "He must have doubled back and smashed the beacon when nobody was looking."

Seth swore and strode several yards away. "We should have left a guard."

But unspoken among them all was the fact that they'd needed every hand to gather wood.

Stopping, Seth planted his hands on his hips, glared up at the violet sky and swore again.

"They'll still find us, won't they?" Willa asked, her voice tremulous. "Please say they'll find us," she added in a little-girl voice that prompted Elizabeth to draw her into her arms as if she were a child to be comforted.

"Shh. Of course, they'll find us," Elizabeth murmured with far more optimism that she felt. "It might take a little longer, that's all."

But when Seth turned to meet her gaze, Elizabeth knew that their predicament had grown far more perilous than any of them could imagine. Not only did they have the weather to contend with, they also had a serial killer who seemed bent on destruction.

A hoarse scream echoed through the clearing, bouncing off the rock face of the cliff.

The hair rose on Liz's nape and she whirled.

"Damn it, now what?" Seth growled.

Automatically, Elizabeth searched the faces around them. "Nealy," she whispered. "Where's Michael Nealy?"

Chapter Ten

Seth started running toward the sound, heading into the trees. Not wanting to be left alone, Elizabeth followed him, her feet slipping in the snow, her breathing becoming labored within a few hundred feet.

Just when she feared that her lungs would explode from the effort to breathe the thin air, Seth came to a skidding halt.

In front of him, rocks bordered a yawning chasm. The slushy rain that had fallen had frozen overnight and a layer of ice made the outcrop slick and hazardous. If not for the way Seth flung an arm around her waist, Liz would have been unable to catch her footing.

"Don't look."

He swung her away from the edge, but not before she caught a glimpse of what lay below. Even from this distance, there was no mistaking the faded double-breasted coat and scuffed sneakers.

That coat. Michael had been so worried about finding his coat. When he'd discovered it while searching for branches, his delight had been contagious.

Michael Nealy.

"Is he...dead?"

"Stay back."

Seth set her well away from the edge—and for once, she was willing to let him protect her. She'd never been any good with heights. What she'd seen had made her dizzy and sick with vertigo...and more. In that brief glimpse she'd been given, she'd noted enough of Nealy's body to know that he was dead.

Seth tried to make his way down the ravine, but when the newly fallen snow gave way to a hidden layer of ice below, he crouched at the edge. After studying the situation, he returned.

"He's gone," he said gravely. "Even if I could get down to him, it wouldn't do any good. He's beyond help."

Liz knew that Seth was couching his words. The injuries to Nealy's skull had been extensive. Blood and gore had all but obscured his features.

Needing to drive away the pictures lingering in her brain, she turned away.

"We can't help him, Liz," Seth said, his arms winding around her waist.

She moved into his warmth, burying her face against his chest.

"How many more?" she whispered, her throat raw with grief. "How many more of us are going to be sacrificed to this damned mountain?"

When Seth didn't immediately answer, she looked up, catching an odd, pensive expression on his features.

"What?" she breathed, sensing that he knew something he wasn't sharing.

He was looking in the direction of the cliff, staring at the snow. It was at that moment that she realized that Nealy's footprints were easy to see—waffle-soled tennis shoes. He'd been wearing waffle-soled tennis shoes.

But next to those prints were the irregular patterns of a larger cheaper brand of sneakers.

Immediately, she began searching the shadows around them. "Frankie did this?"

Seth didn't immediately speak, and Liz shivered. The details that she had been trying so hard to forget began pummeling her consciousness.

Nealy had fallen to his death. Stan had gone into massive convulsions. And Caldwell...

Seth had been so quiet, so ill at ease when he'd returned from wrapping the agent's body in a blanket. The words he'd shouted to Frankie came back to haunt her. Seth had said that Caldwell had been killed.

"What happened to that first FBI agent?" she asked softly. Seth started, and she knew her growing suspicions were correct.

Seth shook his head, then sighed and admitted, "He was shot."

A spasm gripped her stomach and Elizabeth thought she would be sick. All this time, she'd willingly allowed herself to believe that the mountain and the elements were their worst threat. But Frankie Webb was far more sinister. He was a killer who was determined that none of them was ever rescued.

"What about Kowalski?"

"I don't know what happened to Kowalski. He died of massive hemorrhaging, but I'd swear he wasn't injured that badly when I patched him up the night before. He was too lucid for such extensive injuries. But I'm not a doctor, so I have no proof that his death could have been induced."

A shiver coursed up her spine, one that was caused as much by fear as by the cold.

"What do we do now? How can we stop him?"

"Our best bet is a rescue. Beyond that, we're going to have to stay together at all times and be on our guard. After killing Nealy, Webb will probably lie low, but we can't be sure of that."

Just as they couldn't be sure of a rescue, Elizabeth wanted to add.

But she didn't dare say the words out loud.

SHE SPENT most of the evening with Willa and Peter Walsh, trying to keep them both comfortable. Willa was beginning to succumb to the rigors of the cold, and her lapses into childlike confusion were growing more common—making Elizabeth wonder if the woman had hit her head on impact.

"Elizabeth, I've got to find my books," she whispered, tugging on Elizabeth's sleeve.

Elizabeth put down the wet cloth she'd been using

to blot the sweat from Peter's brow. For the hundredth time, she patted Willa's hand, calmed her and then steered her back to her seat.

"They're right there, Willa," Elizabeth said, taking the carefully wrapped diaries from the woman's carry-on bag. Despite all his complaining, Gallegher had spent part of the afternoon sifting through the wreckage until he found Willa's books. In doing so, he'd revealed to Elizabeth that he really did have a sense of compassion buried beneath the layers of unpleasantness.

Willa took the books and lovingly stroked the plastic bags Ricky had provided to protect them from the snow. Her brow creased, and she softly shook her head. A spark of clarity returned to her gaze.

"I'm being such a bother," she whispered, her chin wobbling. "I don't know what's wrong with me.... I just can't seem to…think.…"

Elizabeth squeezed her hand. "Don't you worry. It's the crash. You must have been injured more than we thought. As soon as we're rescued, they'll take you to a hospital."

"I'm just so cold…so…tired."

"Rest for a little while," Elizabeth murmured.

"My books…"

"I'll watch over them."

When she would have straightened, Willa caught her wrist. "Thank you, Elizabeth."

Moments later, she was clearly asleep. Slipping free of Willa's grip, she returned to Peter's side.

"Her color's bad," Peter whispered through parched lips.

"I know. She needs a doctor."

Peter coughed, his whole body shaking with the effort. As he struggled to catch his breath, Elizabeth noted that Willa wasn't the only survivor bearing a sickly color.

"I'm not doing so good, am I?"

She started, then quickly assumed a bland mask. "You're doing fine."

"Liar." His lips twisted at his own inner musings. "I feel like hell, and I'm quite certain I don't look any better."

Searching for something to derail his thoughts, Elizabeth asked, "Did you ever get in touch with your wife?"

Peter's brow furrowed.

"When we met in the terminal, you were trying to phone your wife. You said you'd reached the answering machine instead."

"You have a good memory for details."

"It comes with the job."

"What do you do?"

"I'm in advertising."

His smile was genuine. "Really? Have you developed anything I've seen?"

She sank into one of the seats, drawing her knees against her chest for warmth. "The Meow-Meow Kitty Meow-Meow campaign was mine as well as the Deco Jeans."

Walsh's grin widened. "I've got teenagers at

home who are nuts about that whole brand of clothing. You do your work too well. I can't seem to earn money fast enough to pay for everything...." His words trailed away. Then, in barely a whisper, he said, "I didn't do it."

Elizabeth frowned, wondering if she'd missed something he'd said. "You didn't do what, Peter?"

He sighed, then winced when the action pulled at torn muscles. "There's some money missing at my bank. An auditor is supposed to arrive on Monday. I know enough to guess that they'll point the finger of blame at me. I've got teenagers, I've got bills, and my wife loves to shop. I'm constantly strapped for funds. But I didn't do it."

He took Elizabeth's hand, squeezing her fingers in a painful grip. "If something happens to me—"

"Nothing's going to—"

"Please, just let me finish. If something happens to me, you've got to tell them that I didn't take the money. But I know who did. A few months ago I fired one of my loan officers. He was an old high school buddy in difficult straits and looking for work. From the beginning, he was lousy at the job, but I waited too long to let him go. One day he came to me, resigned and told me he intended to start a career in marketing. Only after he'd left did I begin to find the discrepancies."

He paused for a moment, battling with a series of hacking coughs. "I'd hoped to speak to the auditor and then to my friend. Things will go easier for him if he turns himself in. But if I don't make it back, it would be so much easier for the authorities to pin the crime on a dead man and move on.'' His grasp became painful. ''I can't do that to my wife, my kids. Make sure they know that I loved them.''

His eyes filled with tears. ''That's what I wanted to tell my wife. I was standing there in a crowded terminal listening to my secretary talk about appointments.'' He snorted in disdain.

''Appointments,'' he said in disgust. ''Suddenly I realized that I'd spent far too much time at work over the past few years. I've missed football games and dance recitals and dinner engagements. It's been so long since I've told any of them that I love them and I'm proud of them. I want them to know that.''

He was growing agitated and Elizabeth tried to calm him by patting his arm and murmuring, ''They know, Peter.''

But he became wild, struggling to get up. ''I tried to use my phone once we crashed, but it doesn't work.'' His features crumpled. ''What good are the damn things if they don't work!''

Disturbed by his growing hysteria, she sank onto the floor beside him and drew him into her arms, allowing him to bury his head into her shoulder and sob like a baby.

She was still in that position, patting the man's back when Seth returned. Immediately, her eyes leapt to tangle with his and Peter's words echoed in her ears.

Suddenly I realized that I'd spent far too much

time at work over the past few years.... It's been so long since I've told any of them that I love them....

Her throat tightened and her eyes stung with unshed tears. She'd thrown away her own chance at love. Just like Peter, she'd filled her life with appointments, rather than love.

And it wasn't enough.

It had never been enough.

SHE COULDN'T BREATHE.

Elizabeth lay in the darkness, her eyes wide open. She stared unseeingly into the shadows, her mind focusing over and over again on the broken transmitter.

Why? Why had Frankie Webb destroyed the beacon? It didn't make sense. Surely he had to know that he couldn't survive on the mountain indefinitely. If he'd just thought things through...

She bit her lip. Was that the crux of his problem? Had he snapped? Had he decided that he would rather be dead than captured and that he was willing to sentence them all to the same fate as well?

The grumble of snoring from Ernst Gallegher increased in volume.

I can't breathe. I've got to get out of here.

Frantic for some small amount of space, some measure of privacy she could call her own, Elizabeth carefully shifted away from Seth. She grasped one of the thin blankets, wrapped it around her shoulders, then crawled to the opening and slid into the darkness. Keeping to the inky shadows, she sank into one of the seats Ricky had pulled near to the fuselage and huddled beneath the layers of wool.

Tears crowded close. Hopelessness pressed down on her shoulders, making it impossible to breathe. Her brain ran in frantic circles, trying to find some escape from the situation.

What were they going to do?

"Elizabeth?"

She jumped, a cry escaping her lips as a hand touched her shoulder.

"Hey? What's the matter?" Seth said, concerned.

"What's the *matter?*" she echoed incredulously. One of her arms waved to indicate the wreckage, the darkness and the cold. "What's the *matter?*"

Seth held up his hands in a calming gesture. "Just relax, and—"

"Relax?" She jumped to her feet, her bitter laugh echoing in the cold. "Maybe you can sit back and calmly wait for things to happen, but I can't. My mind keeps racing in circles, searching for a way out. I start to shake every time I hear a noise, hoping it's a plane. Relax? How can I relax when I'm God knows where, marooned with a killer, with no hope of being found?" Her voice rose in a final hysterical note and she clamped her hand over her mouth to keep from sobbing.

"Elizabeth, stop it!" Clasping her upper arms, Seth drew her tightly against him.

She strained against his embrace. The pressure of his thighs against her own was too real. Too wonderful. Struggling to release herself, she tried to ignore the wild delight sweeping through her body, mixing with her terror to create a potent storm of sensation.

Seth cradled her face in his hands, forcing her to look at him.

"They *will* come for us. But we need to be patient. It will be at least forty-eight hours...." He hesitated before adding, "Maybe as much as a week."

"A week," she breathed in disbelief. Seven days—perhaps even more. How was she going to survive another minute?

"I'm telling you the truth because I know you're strong enough to take it."

Seth's words pierced through her silent misery, demanding that she listen to him.

"I need you to help keep the other passengers calm, to reassure them that the time spent waiting is to be expected. Can you do that for me?"

"No, I—"

"*Will* you do that for me?" he amended.

She bit her lip, wishing that she could howl and shout and scream, but knowing that she wouldn't.

Seth needed her help.

He needed her.

The fight seeped from her body, leaving her weak and infinitely weary. She nodded.

"Good girl." Seth looped his arms around her waist, drawing her against him in a loose, comfortable embrace. "I also need you to keep a special eye on Willa. She must have sustained some internal injuries because she's grown pale and weak. She's often disoriented and you're the only person who has developed a real rapport with her.''

''Okay.''

''And Elizabeth…''

She looked up at his shadowy shape in the darkness.

''I really need to kiss you.''

This time, it was she who drew his lips down to hers. The sweetness was instantaneous, filling her with a warmth that was far more satisfying than anything she'd experienced since…

Since the last time she'd been in his arms.

Rising on tiptoe, she deepened the caress. How she'd missed this man. Missed his strength, his adoration, his love.

His own hands tightened around her waist, drawing her up and into him, making her body thrum with a pleasure that was oh, so heady.

''I've missed you,'' she sighed against his lips.

''I'm not going anywhere now.''

''I'm so glad.''

Then there was no more time to whisper. The hunger grew overwhelming, the desire inundating her body. Her fingers dug into his jacket as she strained closer and closer and…

Seth was the first to break away.

''We can't…''

''Why?''

''There's no place for us to be alone.''

She was instantaneously pleased that Seth wanted to continue, and frustrated that he was right. Even the nose section—which might have offered a modicum of shelter—had been compromised by the presence of Frankie Webb.

Seth wrapped his arms around her, drawing her close, tucking her ear against his chest.

The heavy, galloping thud of his heart made her smile. She'd done that to him.

"Why the smile?" Seth asked, his voice rumbling.

"How do you know I'm smiling?"

"I know."

She let the question pass without answering.

"Feeling better?" Seth asked after several long minutes.

"Mmm." She was still cold, still frightened, still worried. But Seth had helped to shoulder the burden and she could go on.

"Thank you," she whispered.

"For what?"

"For everything." She pressed a quick kiss to the hollow of his throat.

The darkness shrouded them in secrecy for several long, precious moments. Then Seth reluctantly stepped away. "We'd better go back."

Elizabeth nodded reluctantly, allowing him to help her inside and settled beside him on the floor. But this time, as she rested her head on his chest and wrapped her arms around his waist, she knew that she would be able to sleep.

"WAKE UP, LIZZIE."

Elizabeth scowled. She was still only partially conscious of her surroundings, but the detested nickname was swiftly drawing her out of her dreams.

"Go 'way," she muttered.

What could the man possibly want anyhow? They were all marooned and would be forced to wait for a rescue. If she chose to spend her time sleeping, how could it be anyone's business but her own?

She felt the whisper of warmth against her ear, and then Seth's low voice. "Either you get up and come with me, or you get to spend the rest of the day here. You can spend hours and hours listening to Ricky's stories and Ernst Gallegher's complaints, just like you've already spent the last two days."

Her eyes immediately popped open. When she'd considered sleeping the day through, she hadn't taken into account that she wouldn't have the shelter to herself.

She tried to sit, but the pounding of her head caused her to moan and she sank back into her makeshift bed.

"You are a cruel, cruel man, Seth."

Squinting against the bright light, she regarded him with her head cocked and her eyes narrowed.

"How can you be so damned chipper?"

"I'm not chipper." He leaned even closer to her ear. "I'm just desperate to escape."

As he backed away, he grinned at her, making it obvious that he wouldn't wait long to see if she bothered to follow him.

As soon as the blanket flapped closed behind him, she ran a hand over her hair—grimacing when she discovered that the tresses had grown even wilder during the night. Grasping her bag, she found her brush, dragged it through the tangled strands and then donned her shoes. Grabbing a couple of candy bars, she dodged outside.

Seth was waiting for her. He leaned against the wing of the plane, one ankle crossed over the other.

Elizabeth jumped to the ground, then hissed as every muscle in her body protested with a giant throb of pain.

He chuckled softly in sympathy. "It gets better," he promised. "You just need to get up and start moving around."

"I hope you're right," she mumbled as she threw him one of the candy bars, then unwrapped her own.

Generally, such a concentrated amount of sugar first thing in the morning made her stomach lurch, but she forced herself to take a bite and ignore the flip-flopping.

"How's the head?" she asked.

He touched a finger to the bandage she'd applied. "Not too bad. How about your bump?"

"It's better, I think." She was trying her best to eat the candy slowly, letting it melt on her tongue before she swallowed. After the previous day's experience with rationing, she knew this was the only meal until late afternoon.

Her stomach rumbled in protest at the thought.

Seth was walking quickly, moving away from the plane. Sun glittered against the snowy valley floor.

The storm clouds that had hovered over them since the crash had disappeared and the sun was dazzling.

"Come on," Seth said, holding out his hand.

"Where are we going?"

"To gather more wood for the signal fire."

She sighed. She should have realized that Seth had ulterior motives in asking for her company.

"What about Webb?"

"We're both armed." Seth's eyes narrowed. "Aren't we?"

She withdrew the derringer from her pocket.

"Keep your eyes open," Seth warned.

"And what am I supposed to do if I see him?"

"Shoot."

She sucked in a quick breath, then coughed when the cold air caught in her lungs.

Seth stroked her cheek with his knuckle. "Aim for his legs if you have to. But we don't have a choice, Liz."

No. They didn't.

Seth drew to a stop at the edge of the first stand of trees. Evergreens grew thickly here, the trees forming a dark impenetrable wall.

Elizabeth shivered, struck by the isolation and the remoteness of their surroundings.

"I didn't think there were any spots like this left on the face of the earth," she murmured, drawing her eyes back to the crisp, clean stretch of snow, rock and pine laid out before her on its snowy canvas. It was almost too beautiful to believe that such a place existed and was not a figment of an artist's imagination.

"I wonder if anyone else has ever been here before us," she mused.

Seth shrugged. "We could be standing on a pile of snow-buried beer cans, for all we know," he observed ruefully.

"Killjoy."

"Realist."

"And I thought you were the dreamer in the relationship."

The silence pounded between them at her choice of words.

"Is that what we're starting here?" Seth asked, his eyes pinning her to the spot. "A relationship?"

She dug her hands into her pockets, then recoiled at the solid shape of the derringer.

"I don't know," she finally admitted.

His lips twitched, then slid into a rueful grin. "Then I suppose I'll have to settle for that much. At least you're thinking about the idea."

At that, he began walking again—leaving her with her mouth open, her heart pounding with something very much like excitement.

Chapter Eleven

"Not like that, Miss Boothe!"

Elizabeth glared at Gallegher over the spicy pine boughs stacked in her arms. In the past hour, he'd appointed himself supervisor of the fuel-finding expedition, and she was getting weary of his comments.

"What do you know?" she retorted under her breath.

For the past few hours, she and Seth had been gathering armloads of pine boughs from the forest. But with the deep snows and an absence of proper tools, progress had been slow and difficult. She was tired. Her body was hot from the activity, while her feet and hands were numb and cold.

Originally, she and Seth had been the only passengers gathering fuel. But some time during their progress, Gallegher had come to join them. He'd left Ricky in the plane to watch over Willa Hawkes and Peter Walsh, both of whom continued to suffer from coughs and low-grade fevers.

Elizabeth sighed in irritation. As if their circumstances weren't rough enough, now they were being plagued by the common cold. Her own head ached and her joints were stiff. No doubt she'd be the next one to succumb.

Wasn't it enough that hunger gnawed at her stomach, and Gallegher's peevishness was grating on her nerves? She'd spent most of the morning resisting the sensation of being watched while her brain tortured her with thoughts of a serial killer stalking her from the shadows. The last thing she needed was a cold.

Or Ernst Gallegher critiquing her work.

Gallegher marched toward her.

"I know enough not to make a signal fire by dumping the wood into a jumbled heap," he said.

The self-righteous edge to his voice echoed against the sharp formations of the cliff. The sun was partially obscured by the puffy clouds forming above the mountain range, throwing a puddle of steel-blue shadow onto the snow around them. Although the darker patch was cooler, it brought a welcome relief from the brilliant white light of sun-drenched snow.

"You've got to be more careful," he said.

"Oh, yeah?"

"Yeah."

"Then you do it," she replied with a sweet smile, calmly dropping the prickly branches on top of his feet.

Gallegher's lips thinned. "Very adult."

"Whatever."

When she turned, it was to find Seth bending to hide his own grin.

She grimaced when Ricky ran toward them from the direction of the plane. "Hey! You haven't seen that woman, have you?"

Elizabeth felt a chill enter her veins. One that had nothing to do with the cold.

"What?"

"Willa Hawkes. She's gone."

"What do you mean she's gone?" Seth asked, his tone ominous.

"Willa wandered off again. She's gone. I thought she might be with you."

Seth swore and turned in a circle, studying the brilliant expanse of snow.

"Which way did she go?"

"I don't know. I was helping Walsh get something to drink. I only turned away for a minute. When I looked up again, she was missing."

Swearing, Seth began running in the opposite direction. Unwilling to allow him to move out of sight, Liz quickly followed. Soon, she saw what had caught his attention. A tiny scrap of color flapped from the tip of a pine bough several yards away. As they shuddered to a halt, Seth snatched Willa's scarf from the bough.

"Where could she have disappeared to?" she asked as Seth examined the valley around them.

He planted his hands on his hips and turned a slow circle, then paused, growing still.

"Stay here."

He began making his way through the fresh drifts. Liz waited in silence, her arms folded together for warmth. Then, after only a few minutes, she hurried after him.

He barely glanced over his shoulder when she approached.

"I told you to stay with the others."

"I can't stay there. I have to do something."

He seemed to understand because he didn't force her to turn around. Soon, she saw what had captured his attention.

Elizabeth's steps slowed and she wished she hadn't been so headstrong. Somehow, she'd expected to find Willa alive. Shaken, yes. Confused, certainly.

But the figure in the snow was still and lifeless and pale.

Slowly, she approached Seth, watching as he hunkered next to the woman and touched her throat with his fingers.

"Is she…"

"She's dead," he whispered huskily.

Although Elizabeth had hardly known the woman, she had to fight to keep from bursting into tears. Damn, damn, damn. How many more lives would be sacrificed before help could come?

Guilt rose in her throat like bile.

"I should have watched her more carefully. I should have brought her with us to gather boughs. I could have tied her to me, if necessary. I could have—"

Her words froze in her throat when Seth stepped

away and she saw Willa clearly for the first time. Despite the ravages of death and cold, there was no denying the stark bruises that wrapped around the woman's throat. Bruises that looked like fingers.

"Seth, she's been—"

He motioned for her to be silent, stopping the statement before it could be uttered. With the barest nod of his head, he indicated that they were no longer alone. Ricky and Gallegher had followed them and were now at the edge of the trees.

"Go back to the plane," Seth called to the men. "There's nothing more we can do for her."

Ricky's chin wobbled. "She's...dead?"

Seth nodded. "Hypothermia."

When Liz would have reacted, he squeezed her hand. "Now get back to the fire before the two of you succumb to the cold as well."

Elizabeth waited until Ricky and Gallegher were out of earshot before asking, "Why didn't you tell them?"

Seth's eyes were narrowed as he tried to plumb the shadows that surrounded them.

"I don't want to start a panic."

"A panic? They already know a serial killer is on the loose."

"Yes. But I don't think they've come to the same conclusion we have. They still think that most of the deaths have other logical explanations."

He looked at her then, his eyes steady and deliberate. And at that moment, Elizabeth knew he was going to put her own worst fears into words.

"We know that Brent Caldwell was shot. Execution-style. But they think he died from injuries sustained in the crash."

"Nealy gets waylaid in the woods—"

"They all think he slipped," Elizabeth interrupted, knowing even as she did so that the man's death couldn't be so easily explained.

"Yes, but we both know he was helped over the edge of that chasm."

She shuddered.

"Stan Kowalski—"

"Stan?" Elizabeth interrupted in confusion. "But he died of internal injuries," she insisted.

"Perhaps. But if that was the case, why didn't he begin to show signs of such trauma earlier? Why did he die nearly twenty-four hours later of something that could be explained much more readily by poisoning?"

"Poisoning?" she breathed. "You think that Webb is responsible for Stan's death as well?"

"You saw the confrontation at the airport. Frankie Webb swore that he would get even with both of those men. From my perspective, it looks like he's done a good job of it."

Seth looked at the prone figure in the snow, his eyes gleaming with sadness. "Now there's Willa. She was a sweet, fragile woman, and she was murdered without cause."

"How is he doing this? He has no real shelter, no food...."

"Maybe he's trying to drive us away from the

plane so that he can have it himself.'' Seth raked his fingers through his hair. ''I don't know. I've tried to analyze the situation from a dozen angles and it doesn't make sense, but I know next to nothing about the psychology of a serial murderer.''

''Webb is out of control,'' Elizabeth whispered. She wrapped her arms around her waist. ''We've got to tell the others everything. They've got to be on their guard.''

Seth took a deep breath, held it, then slowly exhaled. Elizabeth frowned in concern when the sigh ended with a rough cough.

''Fine. I'll trust your instincts. But we'll wait until morning. Maybe the beacon was working long enough to help the authorities pinpoint our location.''

''And after we've told them, what do we do?'' she whispered.

''Pray that someone finds us.''

WHEN ELIZABETH and Seth returned to the shelter, the small space was charged with tension. Peter Walsh lay thrashing in his nest of blankets, mumbling incoherently. Gallegher and Ricky did their best to hold him still, but it wasn't until Elizabeth touched his forehead that Walsh grew quiet, his eyes opening.

''Maureen?'' he asked breathlessly.

Elizabeth looked up at Gallegher and Ricky. ''Maureen must be his wife,'' she said softly.

Ricky took a voluminous handkerchief from his

pocket and coughed into it. "He's been talking about her for hours."

Bending over Walsh, Elizabeth stroked his hair. The man was burning with fever and his body was racked with chills. But as she touched him, the bleariness cleared from his eyes and he shook his head.

"Sorry…Miss Boothe."

"Is Maureen your wife?" she asked with a gentle smile, offering the man some of the melted snow to drink.

He took two swallows, then lay against the cushions in exhaustion.

"No. My eldest daughter. We had an argument six months ago and she…ran away." He clutched the blankets to him and struggled to catch his breath. "She'd gone to stay with…her grandparents… in…Denver." He grimaced. "I was flying out to…apologize…to…beg her to come home."

Elizabeth's heart ached for the man.

"She'll still be there once we're rescued," Elizabeth said, tucking the blankets more securely around his chin.

"I…hope."

THE REST OF THE EVENING passed with agonizing slowness. Ricky and Gallegher huddled over an upended suitcase playing poker with the cards Ricky had unearthed from one of the overhead bins.

"Say, Gallegher, how can you tell if an elephant has been in the refrigerator?"

Gallegher grimaced, but didn't reply.

"There's footprints in the butter!" Ricky laughed uproariously and continued with his repertoire. "How can you tell if an elephant..."

Sinking onto one of the seats, Elizabeth drew her knees close to her chest and wrapped her arms around her knees.

"Walsh is worse," she murmured in a low voice so that only Seth could hear. "He's got a horrible fever, cough, chills...."

Seth swore, squinting through one of the windows as if by sheer force of will he could conjure a rescue plane.

"We're all getting sick," Elizabeth said, stating the obvious. "Gallegher's been complaining of an upset stomach—and since he refuses to eat, I've been willing to believe him. Ricky is wheezing and..."

What she didn't say was that she was beginning to realize that not all of the aches and pains she felt herself were from the crash. For the past few hours, she'd been popping aspirin like candy—without much relief.

Seth rubbed his temples as if he felt an echo of the same throbbing.

"It's to be expected. We're cold, tired, hungry and wet. We'll have to limit our movements more and stay in the shelter as much as we can."

Elizabeth knew that Seth was outlining much the same precautions they would have to take to avoid Frankie Webb. But one of the vital ingredients Seth had left out of the scenario was warmth. With Frankie Webb on the loose, they would not be able to gather wood as efficiently as needed.

She rested her chin on her knees, admitting softly, "I can't do this much longer."

Seth took her hand and wove their fingers together in silent comfort.

Her sigh was even deeper, more heartfelt. If she closed her eyes, she could see the artificial twilight that lingered in the city long after the sun disappeared. She could imagine the warmth of her apartment, the conveniences of a refrigerator stocked with food, soft pillows, a telephone.

"What are you thinking about?" Seth asked quietly.

"Light, heat, food and warmth."

"All the pleasures of home."

Her body thrummed with weariness, but it was her mind and her emotions that seemed strained to the breaking point. If she succumbed to sleep, would she ever be able to summon the energy necessary to meet the challenges tomorrow would bring?

Seth must have sensed her worry because he touched her chin, tilting her face to him.

"Don't worry, Liz. I'll take care of you."

She summoned a shaky smile, but her mind wasn't so easily reassured. She knew Seth would do everything in his power to help them all, but even he couldn't control Frankie Webb.

SETH WATCHED Elizabeth, knowing that her smile was purely for his benefit.

The fact that she was working so hard to keep him from worrying touched him more than he would have ever thought possible. He would have done anything to make that smile real, to lessen the burdens on her heart, to see her returned to the warm safe place she'd been dreaming of.

But there was another part of him that was not quite so selfless. Paradoxically, he dreaded the moment when he and Elizabeth would return to the "real world." Although he knew that their return to civilization needn't signal the end to their suddenly revitalized relationship, somehow he knew that the pressures of her job and a long-distance courtship would weaken whatever inroads they'd made during their hellish experience.

And he didn't want that.

It surprised him how much he'd grown to care for her again in such a short time—but then, maybe he'd never ceased caring for her. After she'd left him, he'd been angry, then bitter, then callously indifferent. But he'd never found a woman who could take her place.

He hadn't even tried.

Elizabeth closed her eyes, and he reached to stroke her hair, hoping to lull her into sleep. As he did so, he found himself wanting—no, needing Elizabeth to be a part of his future. But how? How could they both avoid making the same mistakes?

Granted, they'd both changed over the past few years. They'd matured. And Seth supposed that even their experiences apart had taught them just what they wanted from life—and Seth, for one, didn't want to be alone.

Had Elizabeth reached the same conclusion? He was fairly sure she had. She'd grown so much stronger and independent. When he looked into her eyes, he knew that their close brush with death had caused Lizzie to examine her future more closely than she had ever done before. Moreover, she'd tapped a well of strength that he was sure she'd never suspected she had.

His lips tipped in a wry grimace. They'd both called upon emotional reserves that they hadn't known they possessed. The restlessness that had always seemed to consume Seth had died. When he thought of the time he'd spent with his adventure seeking, it was with a sense of accomplishment and nostalgia. As if that part of his life had been firmly placed in his past.

He wound a curl around his finger. After spending this time with Elizabeth, there was no other woman who could make his heart beat as quickly, his pulse pound as hard, and his breath catch as often.

Yet, even as the desire for adventure faded within him, another desire began to rage. He wanted a home and a family. And even though Elizabeth might label his sudden passion for offspring as simple male conceit, he couldn't push his needs aside. At thirty-six, he suddenly found that he was not willing to wait for a wife and family. He wanted them now. With Elizabeth.

So what was he willing to do to make his dreams

a reality? Would he give up his present life and return to New York?

Seth grew still as the answer slid through his body with a silken warmth.

Yes. He would be willing to do whatever it took, even if that meant sacrificing his needs for hers.

BEFORE SHE'D FALLEN asleep, Liz had agonized over the fact that, come morning, she and Seth would have to tell the others about Webb's involvement in the recent deaths of their companions. She'd dreaded the confrontation and had done her best to forget about it.

But the memory came rushing back early the next morning. She and Seth were still half-asleep when she became aware of a draft. Her eyes flicked open and automatically swept over the interior of the plane. When she discovered that Gallegher and Ricky were missing, she quickly shook Seth awake.

"Seth? Seth! They've gone outside."

Seth was awake in an instant. Swearing, he stumbled from the shelter. Elizabeth automatically followed.

The two men were already halfway across the clearing.

"Gallegher, Ricky! Get back here."

The men stopped, but it was Gallegher who turned, his brow furrowing in irritation.

"Damn it, Brody. Are you going to dictate the call of nature now, too? One of the levers in the plane's lavatory is jammed and I don't want to wait until someone can fix it.''

Seth's gaze was already scanning the trees.

"We need to talk.''

"In a minute,'' Ricky said with a grin.

"There are some things that can't be controlled, Brody,'' Gallegher called.

"Listen, Gallegher, this is neither the time or the place to argue. Frankie Webb is out there and—''

"I don't give a damn about that prisoner anymore. He's probably frozen to death.''

"Gallegher!'' Elizabeth shouted when the men began walking again. "Nealy didn't fall off that cliff, he was pushed. And Willa Hawkes was strangled.''

The two men halted in stunned disbelief, then Gallegher turned, his eyes narrowed. "So what are you saying? That we've got some psychotic serial killer *hunting* us?''

Seth's lips thinned in irritation. "Keep your voice down.''

Gallegher's features grew florid. "Keep my voice down? Who the hell cares how loud I talk? We're alone on this godforsaken mountain. Don't you get it? No one can hear us. No one!''

"That doesn't mean that we should abandon all reason,'' Elizabeth said placatingly.

"And why the hell not? I've been calm and rational since we crashed, and what has it got me? Absolutely nothing—despite the fact that the man running around loose was responsible for killing my daughter!''

They all stared at him, stunned.

He stomped forward, his face growing mottled and red. "Don't you see? I didn't come on this little junket for a vacation? I came to kill the man. I came to end his life the way he ended my Valerie's. I even managed to slip a gun onto the plane by dressing in a pair of coveralls and pretending to be a maintenance man. I had two bullets in the chamber. One for Webb and one for me."

He pointed accusingly at Seth. "Then this idiot crashed into a mountainside and my daughter's killer was allowed to run free—*free,* damn it."

Gallegher was screaming now. "You took my gun, didn't you? You took my gun and hid it!"

Seth shook his head, holding up his palms in a calming gesture. "I don't know what you're talking about."

"I don't believe you! For all I know, you're in league with Frankie Webb and this crash is some elaborate scheme he's concocted in order to escape. One by one, you're picking us off so there won't be any witnesses to what's happened."

He was growing wild, his words disjointed and illogical. "Is that it? Is he manufacturing his own death so that he can assume some new identity? Is that why you're after us? Why you're all after us?"

His laugh caused gooseflesh to pebble Elizabeth's skin.

"Well, it won't work, you hear me? I won't die! I won't give that man the satisfaction. I will survive this ordeal and hunt him down myself. Then I'll come after you." He shook a finger in Seth's direction.

"Gallegher," Ricky rasped, touching his arm.

The big man jerked away as if burned. "Don't you touch me, you fool. Can't you see that *he's* the reason we're here?"

Gallegher waved his arm accusingly. "He's responsible for the plane that brought us here. It's his incompetence that resulted in the crash. Then, rather than waking up and smelling the coffee, we allowed him to take charge."

He began pacing in agitation. "Don't you see? We've been blindly following him—like sheep to the slaughter. And he doesn't know Jack Squat about anything! We never should have listened to him in the first place. We've been sitting on our butts waiting for a rescue when he knows damn well that a rescue is never coming. By this time we could have walked out of these mountains!"

"To where?" Elizabeth asked pointedly.

"To civilization, to a cabin, to a road—anywhere but to the certain death that we'll find here."

"Calm down, Gallegher," Seth said, his voice low and firm.

"Calm down! I think it's time that we all got a little upset. Don't you see? We're nothing but sitting ducks here—and we've got a killer picking us off one by one. We've got to gather our things and start walking!" Gallegher's eyes were growing wild, his skin gleaming with sweat, spittle flying from his mouth as he spoke.

Elizabeth met Seth's gaze and quickly decided that the man was growing hysterical. Something had to be done—now—before he lost complete control.

"Let's sit down and talk things through, Mr.—"

Elizabeth wasn't allowed to finish her statement. Gallegher whirled on her next, shaking a finger in her direction.

"And why should I listen to you? You're nothing but this man's mistress, his—"

"Enough!" Seth shouted. His voice echoed in the winter stillness. "It's time for you to take a deep breath and—"

A shot exploded in the clearing.

Elizabeth jumped, automatically whirling toward the trees where the sound had originated. There was a flash of shadow, and then a shape began fleeing through the trees.

She turned to look at Seth, then at Ernst Gallegher, who had fallen lifeless to the snow. The engineer had been shot between the eyes. Blood spattered the snow behind him, the icy crystals absorbing the puddle oozing from his skull.

"Where'd he get a gun?" Elizabeth whispered, then said again, her voice rising. "Where did Webb get a gun?"

"He must have found the one Gallegher stashed on the plane," Seth growled.

The air became suddenly charged with tension.

"He's been watching us all this time," Ricky whispered. "He's been playing with us, toying with us, waiting for us to drop our guard."

"Get back in the plane," Seth shouted, already turning in the direction of the fleeing shape.

"Seth, no!"

Terrified, Elizabeth turned to Ricky. "You've got to stop him. Webb will kill him if Seth catches up to him. Please!"

Ricky thundered after Seth, finally managing to halt him with a flying tackle.

"Stop!" Ricky shouted when Seth tried to wrestle free. "He'll only kill you, and without your help, we all die."

The words must have penetrated the fog of Seth's brain, because he grew suddenly still, his gaze sweeping to meet Elizabeth's. Then, visibly, the fight drained from his body and he collapsed in the snow.

"Get back in the plane. Hurry!" he said urgently. "From now on, no one leaves the shelter during the daytime. After dark, if we stay away from the light of the fire, we can probably stay to the shadows and stretch our legs—but no one goes out alone. No one."

He rolled to his feet and extended a hand to help Ricky.

Another shot exploded in the silence. Ricky yelped and fell back in the snow, clutching a hand to his chest.

As Seth lunged to throw Elizabeth to the ground, a roar of rage echoed through the clearing from the direction of the trees.

"Two bullets," Elizabeth said, meeting Seth's

horrified gaze. "Gallegher said he loaded his gun with only two bullets."

Cautiously, Seth looked up, then stood and pulled Elizabeth to her feet.

"Come on. We've got to get Ricky to the plane and stop the bleeding."

IT WAS PAST MIDNIGHT when Seth shoved his hands into his pockets, huddling deeper into his coat to ward off the frigid bite of the wind sweeping down over the cliff. Restlessly, he scanned the indigo skyline, searching for the faintest glimmer of light.

By now, a search operation would have been activated. There was no doubt someone was looking for them—and would eventually find them. The only question was when.

And whether their rescuers would arrive in time.

Already, Walsh was delirious from whatever unknown injuries had been plaguing him. And Ricky...

Ricky was doing his best to keep a brave front, but he'd lost a lot of blood and his lungs rattled from his efforts to breathe.

The flap twitched and Elizabeth jumped into the snow.

"I thought you were sleeping," Seth said.

She shook her head. "I can't seem to do more than doze for a few minutes at a time." She cast a nervous glance around the clearing. "Do you think it's safe to stay out here by the fire?"

"For a few minutes. Webb must have found the gun Gallegher hid. Gallegher said it only had two bullets. If he'd had a full clip, we'd all be dead right now."

Her eyes were dark and luminous. "But a lack of ammunition won't stop him, will it?"

Seth shook his head. "I doubt it."

She clutched the collar of her coat beneath her chin.

"Are Walsh and Ricky asleep?" Seth asked after a few minutes of silence.

She shook her head. "For the moment. They're restless."

"And what about you? How are you doing?"

She stiffened. "Me?"

"You've been taking a lot of aspirin."

She grimaced. "You miss nothing."

He grinned. "Headache?"

She nodded. "Headache, body ache…you name it."

"We'll take it easy the next couple of days."

Take it easy. Even he knew the statement was nothing more than a euphemism for "wait."

"Come here," he murmured, holding out his arms and folding her into his embrace.

She stepped willingly closer, tucking her head beneath his chin.

"Seth?"

"Mmm." He found it hard to concentrate. She felt so good in his arms, so right.

"Thank you," she said against his chest.

"For what?"

"For getting us this far. And for being here for me."

Being here for her. He hadn't been there during their marriage.

He'd been wrong. So very wrong.

Bending, he placed a kiss on the top of her head. "We'll get through this, Elizabeth. Together, we'll find a way."

Chapter Twelve

It was dark when Elizabeth awoke and eased out of Seth's embrace. Stretching, she slipped outside into the cool evening air.

She knew she was being foolish—and she knew that Seth would chastise her for leaving the safety of the plane. But she needed a minute to herself, and the fire that had been going all day had completely died. Not even a glowing ember remained to reveal her presence.

Holding her arms over her head, she breathed deeply of the dark evening air and filled her lungs with the crisp, clean drafts. Daring to press her disobedience even further, she ambled a few feet in the direction of the distant pines. The exercise helped to ease the stiffness out of her muscles and clear her brain. She paced back to the plane, then paced away again.

She would continue exercising for a minute. Just a minute.

Humming softly to herself, she bent to grab a

handful of snow, shaping it into a ball and tossing it toward the trees. It landed with a sullen plop several yards short of the forest. Grimacing, she bent to grab another handful, pausing when she seemed to hear the pines sighing in commiseration.

Enjoying the brief freedom, she wound up for another throw. This time, her missile skittered through the tops of the trees, scattering the snow from the heavy branches. The forest hummed an accolade and she playfully curtsied to receive their praise.

"Thank you, thank you, than—"

She broke off, whirling around, her eyes scanning the heavens.

Humming. She wasn't imagining anything. The humming was real.

"Seth!" Her feet slipped in the snow as she raced toward the plane.

"Seth! Ricky! Peter! Come quick!"

SETH'S HEAD jerked up. A shudder ran though his body like a chilling wave.

"Seth!"

The terrifying scream came again.

Lunging to his feet, he crossed the width of the fuselage and stumbled outside. Almost immediately, he spotted Elizabeth running toward him, her hair flying out behind her like a tangled banner.

He rushed toward her, his heart pounding, his breath coming in labored pants. Damn! What was she doing outside on her own? Was the woman insane?

He came to a skidding stop, his hands gripping her

forearms as she barreled into him. A quick sweeping search convinced him that there were no obvious signs of blood or broken bones. But even as he tried to pull her into his arms, she yanked away.

"Seth, listen!"

"What?"

"Listen!"

Seth couldn't hear anything but the pounding rush of his pulse beating in his ears.

"Can you hear it?"

He cocked his head, struggling to determine what had startled her.

"A plane," she gasped just as he caught the faint, throbbing hum. "It's a plane!"

He sucked in a breath of air and held it in silent prayer as he scanned the skyline, straining to pinpoint the source of the faint sound.

"Get the box of matches and the flares!"

The order was issued even as he raced toward the wing where they had stored the bucket of fuel. "They should be able to see a fire for miles at this time of night!"

Elizabeth was already running. Heaving herself inside, she hurried to the orange nylon bag. For several precious seconds she fought with a zipper that had grown cold and stiff.

Finally, the fastener yielded enough for her to fit her hand into the opening. Her fingers shook with excitement as she dug inside for the matches. Over and over again, the container eluded her grasp, sinking toward the bottom of the bag. The box seemed to be playing some horribly mocking game, refusing to cooperate.

"Please," she whispered desperately under her breath. "Please don't do this."

Her fingers finally found the matches. In a flash she was whirling around and leaping into the snow.

"I've got them!" she shouted to Seth who was sloshing the fuel onto the pile of branches and boughs.

Stumbling, she nearly dropped the box into the snow before she recovered herself and came to a gasping, shuddering halt just in front of him.

"Good girl!" He took the box from her fingers, handing her the bucket. Half of the fuel still remained inside the plastic container.

"Take this back to the plane. If this doesn't work, we may need it later." His head was bent over the mound of boughs, but his eyes lifted to stab her with a piercing warning.

She nodded, pressing a hand against the stitch in her side. "It's going to work," she insisted breathlessly. "It has to."

For one brief moment, their eyes met and held. After so many endless days spent waiting for rescue, they barely dared to hope that an end was actually within reach.

"Cross your fingers," Seth murmured.

She laughed shakily. "And my toes!"

Backing away, she clutched the bucket handle in both hands until the metal handle pressed painfully through her gloves. Her heart was slamming in her chest as she watched him hunch over the wood.

A shiver ran down her spine as the match rasped over the side of the box, sputtering to life. A gust of wind doused the tip before it could touch the pile of boughs.

Once again, a match grated against the side of the box. A quick breath of wind blew it out. Again and again, Seth tried to light the matches, throwing them into the snow when the tips were unable to withstand the wind long enough to ignite the jet fuel.

Elizabeth glanced apprehensively at the horizon, seeking a betraying glimmer of light before her eyes jumped convulsively toward the mound of glistening boughs. Her frustration mounted to a fever point. She had to clench her teeth to keep from screaming aloud.

The signal fire had to light! It had to! This might be their only chance to get off this horrible mountain alive.

"Damn it, where are the flares?" Seth demanded as once again the match refused to stay lighted.

Her heart slammed into her throat. "I left them in the plane." She slipped in the snow as she spun around.

"Never mind. There's no time," he yelled after she had only taken a few steps.

Finally, one match grew braver than the others, glowing brightly in the dusky evening light. Seth dropped it into the pile of evergreen boughs. In a whooshing explosion of light and sparks, the signal fire spread through the trails of fuel, growing into a roaring, gyrating blaze.

They both turned toward the sound they had heard, praying that it would grow stronger.

"Please," Elizabeth whispered aloud, trying to discern a speck of movement on the horizon.

"There it is!" Seth loped toward her, drawing her against his chest. He pointed to the gleaming flashes of color that marked the path of the distant aircraft. Then his arms dropped to tightly encircle her waist.

"They'll see us, Lizzie. All they have to do is look this way."

The plane was a tiny dot in the distance, barely visible except for the flashing dots of red and green that marked its path toward a distant range of mountains. Elizabeth shuddered softly. The aircraft wavered slightly from its path, moving toward them.

Seth's arms tightened around her chest, crushing her against him. Elizabeth could feel Seth's heart slamming against the wall of his chest. Its wild rhythm was only half of what hers seemed to be as her hands clenched expectantly around the muscles of his forearms.

Behind them, the fire crackled and grumbled in protest, emitting a shower of sparks that shot up into the black velvet air.

Surely the pilot had seen the blaze! Surely they would all be rescued.

Elizabeth focused on that one thought—rescue, rescue, rescue.

Squinting, she tried to note any changes in the

craft's flight. Something had made the pilot change the course he'd been taking. So why didn't the lights seem to come any closer?

Mentally, Elizabeth willed the occupants to notice them. If her thoughts could be transmitted through space and time, she prayed that someone would hear her inner cries and sense her panic and anticipation. But the plane seemed to hang suspended in an inky, ebony sky.

Then she sank her teeth into her lip when the plane eased back to its original course.

"No," she whispered, then more loudly, "No! Come back! Come back!"

Behind her, Seth grew still, the hold around her waist growing lax.

"It's no good, Elizabeth." His voice was low and weary.

"What do you mean?" she demanded helplessly, jerking around to glare at him.

His eyes grew sad. "The lights are heading away from us. Even if it was a search plane, they won't be back until morning."

"No!" Her vision began to swim and blur. "No, they can't do that!"

"They're gone," he whispered.

The twinkling pinpricks of color disappeared behind a distant mountain peak.

"But…" Elizabeth grew numb, disbelief acridly tainting her tongue. "No. They have to come back. They have to…"

The blinking lights did not reappear.

Her shoulders sagged. Her mouth grew dry. She was suddenly haunted by all the wasted effort—the fuel, the heavy pile of boughs, the matches. Things that they couldn't afford to lose.

A bitter lump lodged in her throat. How could the unseen crew of that plane do this to them? Hadn't they noticed the brilliant light? Hadn't they heard her mental pleas for assistance? Hadn't they known?

Slowly, carefully, Elizabeth eased out of Seth's embrace. Biting her lip to keep from sobbing aloud, she bent and secured the lid on the bucket. Then she moved toward the wing of the plane, her steps heavy. Using every last ounce of strength she possessed, she swung the bucket under the battered metal, stowing it carefully in its nest of snow. Then she returned to the warmth of the blazing fire, finding little comfort in its heat.

"There will be other planes, Elizabeth."

She gazed at Seth over the leaping conflagration. "What if there aren't any more planes, Seth? What if we die on this hulking mountain and no one finds us until the hot summer sun begins to bleach our bones?"

"Lizzie, stop it!"

"No, you stop it, Seth!" When he moved toward her, she halted him with an impatient gesture of her hand. "Our supplies won't last until spring. They won't even last two weeks. What if a search plane never comes? Then what do we do?"

"I guess we make the best of it," he finally stated.

Her laugh was bitter.

"Make the best of it? How can I make the best of my death when I made a royal mess of my life! I can't simply bow out gracefully without a fight."

He planted his hands on his hips. "Then what do you want, Lizzie? What do you want me to say?"

"I don't know what I want you to say," she lashed out. "But I won't die when these feelings are tearing me apart inside."

"What feelings?" He stepped nearer to the flames, the light slipping into the hollows of his face to illuminate the intensity of his gaze.

"Don't you see? I'm falling into the same trap, the same emotions. I'm beginning to...depend on you again."

He became very still, his features growing unreadable.

"Is that so awful?"

"Yes," she sobbed. "When we split up I *found* myself. I became independent and strong. I learned to rely on my own wits and ambitions to make me happy. But now, I'm coming dangerously close to surrendering everything to you again."

He shook his head and walked resolutely around the edge of the fire.

"Not surrendering. Sharing."

"What's the difference?"

When she would have dodged out of reach, he caught her and pulled her close.

"The difference is in the intent. You're right. When we were married you looked to me for everything that you thought your life was lacking—and I failed you. I know that now. I should have opened up to you more, I should have taken the time to really know you.''

He cradled her face in his hands. "But we're different now.''

"Not really.''

"Yes. Really. You've learned what it means to stand up for yourself. You knew what you wanted from life, and when I didn't measure up to your expectations, you risked everything to pursue your own future. And maybe it sounds crazy, but I'm proud of you for what you did. It's taken me years to realize this, but I was out of line. I deserved everything you said. I deserved to lose you.''

He bent low, forcing her to meet the intensity of his gaze. "But I also learned a few things about myself during the separation. I learned how bleak life can be when a person is alone. I don't want to be alone any longer. I'm also smart enough to realize that the spot you left in my life can't be filled by anyone but you.''

Elizabeth took a deep, bracing breath. "What are you saying?''

"That I want you to think about us. Carefully. I want you to seriously consider if there's room for me in your life.''

She shook her head. "I don't see how we can possibly—''

He laid his finger over her lips. "Don't think about the practicalities or the difficulties. Not now. Not yet.

Just think about us. Have we reached a point where we could try again?''

Before she could speak, he turned her in his arms so that they could both stare into the rollicking flames.

''Don't say anything more about this until morning,'' he whispered. ''Think about it. Just think about it.''

He sank into one of the battered seats, pulling her into his embrace. For long moments, she lay in the circle of his arms, her body absorbing the heat of the fire and more. Suddenly, she realized that despite the circumstances, the disappointment and the heartache, she felt safe in this man's arms. Safe. Needed.

Whole.

She could give him the answer he needed now, she realized. As much as she might bluster and hesitate, there was no escaping the stark truth.

She'd fallen in love with Seth Brody.

Again.

''Tomorrow we'll start over,'' Seth said.

For a moment, she thought that he'd read her mind, but then she realized that he was referring to the fire.

Her heart ached as she eyed the branches that would continue to burn until morning. It had taken all day and several people to gather the supply of wood. With only four survivors left—and only two of them mobile—how long would it take to gather fuel for the next signal fire?

And the next and the next? she wondered wearily.

Choking back her self-defeating attitude, she took a deep, bracing breath. She was tired, that's all. If necessary, she would gather wood for a hundred fires!

"Maybe we should get Walsh and Ricky," she whispered. "The warmth would do them good—and after all the noise we've made, I'm sure they're wondering what has happened."

Seth bent to press a kiss against her ear. "Sure."

Taking her hand, he led her back to the plane and helped her inside, then climbed up himself.

"Ricky? Peter? How are you feeling?" Elizabeth called. "Do you think you could make it outside? We've got a fire going and…"

The words died in her throat when she peered into the shadows. Ricky had fallen into the aisle. Blood ran from his nose and ears and his hands reached silently toward the doorway.

"Dear God," Elizabeth whispered.

Seth hurried to kneel beside the man, pressing his finger against Ricky's throat.

"He's dead," he said, his voice choked.

Chapter Thirteen

Seth insisted that they wait until morning to begin gathering more wood for a signal fire. This time, with only two of them able to work, and the forest already raided in the spots nearest the plane, the task was slow and painstaking. Their only comfort lay in the fact that with each trip back to the shelter, they could stop and rest near to the fire kept burning next to the fuselage.

As they trudged along the path they'd broken, Seth knew that it was those same thoughts of the fire that pushed Elizabeth forward as they returned from their fifth trip of foraging. As she and Seth stumbled into the trampled snow near the shelter, he noted that her arms were quivering from the effort it took to carry her load of branches.

Moaning, she bent, dropping her boughs into the snow near the battered tail section. Judging by her pained expression, her arms and hands throbbed as she straightened them to her sides.

Seth hunkered low, dropping his own load beside

hers. Then he pushed himself to his feet, grunting softly, deep in his throat. Placing his hands on his hips, he arched his back, closing his eyes with a weary sigh.

"How many more trips?" Elizabeth asked, breathing heavily.

Seth wanted to tell her they were finished, that they'd gathered more than enough wood, but they still had a full day of work ahead of them if they were to replace the supply of boughs the fire had already consumed.

"A few," he offered noncommittally.

She sank into one of the seats and held her hands out to the blaze. He grimaced to himself when he noted that her palms were blistered and scratched.

Damn. Why hadn't he thought about her hands? Why hadn't she complained?

Jumping into the plane, he approached the body they'd covered in a blanket. They needed to move Ricky outside to where the other victims had been taken, but Seth had wanted to wait until they had a supply of wood.

Swearing at what he was about to do—what he felt compelled to do—Seth reached beneath the blanket and slid Ricky's fur-lined gloves from the man's hands.

"I'm sorry, Rick," he whispered as if the man regretted the loss. Then Seth grabbed the man's sample case and hurried back into the sunshine.

ELIZABETH HELD her face up to the weak sunshine. The sun was riding high, filling the clearing with its brilliant light.

Since time was of the essence in gathering more fuel for a signal fire, she and Seth had both decided to begin their task at dawn. Even so, Elizabeth found it hard to convince herself to get moving. She'd wanted to spend the day sleeping next to the warmth of the failed signal fire.

"Here. You may as well use these."

Elizabeth stared at the fur-lined mittens that Seth extended toward her. An eternity seemed to have passed since that day when she'd regarded Sticky Ricky's gloves so enviously. Now that they were being offered to her, she didn't think that she could use them.

"You've got to keep warm," Seth insisted. "No one would begrudge you their use."

Although her fingers were cold and her hands rough and chapped, she still couldn't bring herself to take them.

Seth must have sensed the reason for her hesitation because he relented. Taking his own leather gloves from his jacket pocket, he gave them to her, then struggled to pull Ricky's mittens over his larger hands.

Although the worn leather of Seth's gloves would never prove as warm as the others, Elizabeth willingly took them.

"Now for his case."

Elizabeth's stomach growled. Over the past few days, it had occurred to her more than once that

Sticky Ricky's samples case could be filled with food and drink. But now that Seth had found the case beneath a pile of snow near the tail section and the moment had come to open it, she hesitated. It was wrong to go through Ricky's things like this. They should show more respect for the dead.

But the dead were not in need of food, she reminded herself forcefully.

Setting her chin on her bent knees, she watched as Seth used a screwdriver to pry at the locks. At long last, they ripped free.

"Here goes," Seth murmured, then flipped the lid open.

Several seconds passed before Elizabeth was able to absorb the sight that confronted her. The samples case was filled with cookies, dozens and dozens of cookies.

"What the hell?" Seth whispered.

Elizabeth was the first to move. On top of the plastic bags of cookies was a single manila envelope. Prying the brads open, she removed a single slip of paper.

"It's a recipe." Her eyes widened. "It's for Mrs. Walker's Chocolate Chip Cookies."

They looked at one another, then began to laugh. Somehow, Sticky Ricky had stolen the most closely guarded secret in the food business.

But their laughter soon faded and Elizabeth fought to swallow past the tightness in her throat. Seth must have felt the same sadness that inundated her body, because he closed the lid, then removed the mittens and laid them on top of the case.

"Poor Ricky," she sighed.

Poor Ricky and Stan. Willa, Caldwell, Nealy and Gallegher.

How many more would be added to the list before this ordeal was over?

THEY MADE TWO more trips before Seth ordered another rest period and they collapsed near the dying fire.

Seth eyed Elizabeth in concern, knowing that, emotionally and physically, she was swiftly reaching a breaking point.

"Come here," he said, holding his arms wide.

She willingly shifted onto the ground beside him, allowing him to hold her close.

Sighing, he stroked her hair and studied her upturned features. Even now, with her skin half-tanned and half-burned from the sun and bitterly cold wind, and her eyes circled with ridiculous raccoonlike markings, she was beautiful. How could he ever have forgotten how lovely she was? How could he have forgotten the dark captivating spell of her eyes?

How could he ever let her go if she asked him to leave her alone?

"Lizzie, we need to talk." Seth spoke quickly, his voice tight as he stared down at the tousled waves twining around his fingers. The time had come to tell her how much he loved her. He couldn't put it off another moment. He'd learned from his mistakes—and one of his biggest mistakes during their brief marriage had been his unwillingness to put his feelings into words.

"Oh, Seth, I'm sorry." She sighed. "But I'm just too tired and discouraged to hold up my end of the conversation." Her lips twisted ruefully. "And I'm afraid I wouldn't make much sense out of your end, either."

Her weary tone made him smile. The warmth of her body filled him with such pleasure, such joy.

"You do look tired," he murmured, one lean finger reaching out to stroke the velvety curve of her cheek. He frowned when he discovered that her skin was hot and dry to the touch.

"You've been working too hard," he said. "Make sure you get something to drink. I don't want you getting dehydrated on me."

"I will." But her voice was a mere sigh.

He slid his fingers through her hair, tipping her head so that he met the dark velvet of her gaze. "Even when you're exhausted, you're the most beautiful woman I've ever known."

She gazed at him with tortured eyes, as if fearing his words had been wrenched from the hardships they'd suffered during the past few days—when in reality, their situation had forced him to look at what he would be without her.

"You are so precious to me," he whispered, past the sudden thickening of his chest.

Reaching up, she circled one wrist to pull his hand from her hair.

"So are..." She broke off when the dancing light illuminated the broken skin of his hands.

"Oh, Seth." She sighed painfully, pulling his other hand free so that she could study them both in the weak winter sun. "Your hands..."

She darted a glance from his palms to the firm contours of his face and jaw. Bending her head, she tenderly placed a kiss in the center of each palm, her lips easing the ache of his abused flesh even in that brief brushing caress. "I'm so sorry." Her apology was choked.

Crooking his finger beneath her chin, he forced her to meet his gaze.

"Tears? For me?"

She turned away from him as if ashamed of the sudden emotions that had forced her to surrender to such a useless feminine weakness.

"For you. For us," she stated.

Once again, he forced her to look at him.

"What makes you cry for us?"

Yanking away from the intensity of his stare, she fiercely scrubbed away the dampness on her cheek. But as soon as she wiped away the tears, others followed.

Seth swallowed the tightness closing around his throat. Through this entire ordeal, Elizabeth had risen to every challenge. She had a backbone of pure steel when she needed it.

Yet the sight of his hands had brought her to tears.

"I love you, Lizzie," he whispered, knowing he couldn't hold on to the words any longer.

Elizabeth lifted her head to stare at him, tears still filling her eyes.

"Don't," she whispered.

"Don't love you?"

She shook her head. "Don't tell me that you love me. Not here. Not like this. So much has happened...so much is still unresolved."

"My feelings aren't going to change." He took her chin, lifting it so that he could look deeply into her eyes and challenge her own uncertainty. "My feelings have never changed. I love you today as much or more than the day we married."

When she would have spoken and voiced her doubts again, he placed a finger on her lips.

"But I can wait. I can wait until we've been rescued and until you're ready to accept that things never died between us. Our relationship was merely...interrupted."

She move several feet away from him. It was obvious that she was trying to appear unaffected. But he knew her emotions weren't casual. She loved him. She had always loved him. But she didn't trust her emotions.

He wanted to hold her, make love with her. But he wouldn't give in to his needs. Not yet. Once before, he had rushed things—and his impatience had resulted in their marriage lasting less time than most couple's courtships.

Slowly, his hands clenched into tight fists despite the shooting sparks of pain that shot up his arms. Turning his head, he studied the too-familiar features exposed to the silvery haze of the sun. She was beautiful. The light lovingly traced the delicate features of her face, outlining the soft, womanly curves of her body with a caressing touch he wished to imitate. Even her hair gleamed, capturing the reddish hues of the crackling fire and reflecting them back again with an electric brilliance.

His eyes returned to the raw skin of his hands.

Holding his palms out to the fire, he bit back a groan when the warmth restored the feeling to the numbed flesh and sent a prickling sensation through his skin. His fingers twitched uncontrollably.

Damn, he was tired, he thought, resisting the temptation to lie back in the snow and close his eyes. His body ached with fatigue. His lungs felt tight as if he were getting a cold, and his head pounded. He could only guess how Elizabeth had managed to withstand the strain of the past few hours.

Sighing heavily, he filled his empty lungs with the pungent smell of pine, hoping it would revitalize him. Instead, it seemed to seep through his body like potent incense, leaving him weary and relaxed.

Elizabeth shifted to retrieve the melted snow near the fire. He saw her wince as she drank and wondered if her throat was as raw and scratchy as his own.

Drawing his legs up to his chest, he extended his arms over his knees, dropping his head onto the pillow formed by his elbows. They were both feeling the effects of the cold and the weather, he realized. But, on his own part, he feared it was the mental weariness that threatened to undermine him the most. Last night's near-rescue, Ricky's death and their efforts to replenish the signal fire had taken more out of him than he had realized. He was tired of it all— tired of chocolate chip cookies for breakfast, tired of snow, tired of being cold and wet and sleeping in a half-sitting position. His body ached, his chest was tight. And his head...if only he could rid himself of the pounding....

"We'd better go after another load," Elizabeth said, sighing, and he realized she was right. If he continued to sit for much longer, he wouldn't be going anywhere.

"I'll just check on Walsh," she said.

When she disappeared into the fuselage, he took three aspirin from his pocket and washed them down with some of the melted snow. He'd taken the same amount of medication barely two hours earlier, without feeling much relief. Hopefully the double dose would ease the pounding pressure.

"Ready?" Elizabeth asked as she jumped down.

"How's Walsh?"

She shrugged, but there was no denying that she was worried. "The same. Feverish, delirious. He's wasting away and I don't know what to do for him."

Seth took her hand and squeezed. "Pray for a rescue. That's the only thing that can help him now."

"I worry about leaving him here alone," she said, glancing at the dark tree line.

"I know. But with the supplies Webb stole, he seems content to stay away from us for a while. Either that, or he's found a nice hidey-hole and he doesn't feel inclined to leave it.'' He grimaced. ''In any event, I doubt he'd go after Walsh. There's no sport in killing a dying man.''

He moved to wrap her in his arms. ''Just watch your back. The man's cold, hungry and desperate. Up until now, he's been picking off the passengers one by one. But he's never touched you—his most likely target.''

Elizabeth had thought the same thing more than once. ''Why? Why has he left me alone?''

There was a pause and she felt the stiffening of his body.

''My guess is that he's saving his best victim for last.''

THE TRIP INTO THE FOREST was numbing, the gathering of the branches excruciating. Several times, when Seth's back was turned, Elizabeth sneaked an aspirin out of her pocket and did her best to swallow it without the aid of water. By the time she'd taken four and was reaching for the fifth, she was reminded of the consequences of overmedicating herself once before. She was beginning to believe that nothing would ease the pounding of her head and the rawness of her throat. As much as she might try to deny the evidence of her own body, she was coming down with a cold, or the flu or worse. She wanted little more than to curl up in Seth's whispered confession.

He loved her.

Despite her weariness, she felt a tingling invade

her limbs. *He loved her still.* And as much as she tried to caution herself against trusting her emotions during this ordeal, she knew she loved him, too. She'd always loved him. But she had also learned that love wasn't always enough. Once before, she and Seth had failed to meet the challenges of everyday living. What would happen to them when they got off this mountain?

If they got off this mountain....

"That's enough for today," Seth said from his position a few feet away.

Elizabeth was fully aware that the statement was made for her benefit. They didn't have nearly the number of branches that they'd used the night before—and if they kept the fire burning, they would need even more.

But she was suddenly too weary to argue. Maybe if she slept for a few hours, she could rally her energy.

"Once we're back at the plane, we should..."

He broke off, a sudden stillness freezing his features.

An icy wave of confusion and concern plummeted to the pit of her stomach.

"What is it?" she asked fearfully as he brushed past her, pushing his way through the snow. "Seth?"

He didn't seem to hear her as he walked away from the trees to a slight clearing a few yards away. Then he stopped, his arm lifting as he shielded the sun from his eyes, scanning the brilliant blue of the sky. She shuddered when she caught the barely audible curse that he muttered through clenched teeth.

"What's—"

"Get the mirror." He was already running in the direction of the plane.

Confused, she followed him more from instinct than from any strength of will.

"Seth?"

"Get the mirror and meet me in the center of the clearing."

Elizabeth ran still unsure what had caused Seth to behave so alarmingly. Then she heard it. The throbbing purr of an approaching plane.

"Where…is it…coming from?" she gasped, pressing a hand to her side.

Seth whirled, loping backward and scouring the sky with his eyes. "I'm not sure." He urged her on with a wave of his arm. "Hurry!"

"But the fire!"

"There's no time. Get the mirror!"

Her feet skidded in the snow before she gained enough traction to move. She crossed the last hundred yards with more strength and speed than she ever would have thought possible.

Leaping into the jet, she darted toward the orange nylon bag, grabbing it by the straps and whirling out of the plane. As she ran, her hand dug into the contents. Without any of the fumbling she had encountered the night before, her fingers curled around the shiny glass.

Racing toward the spot where Seth stood in the

brightest patch of sunlight, she handed him the mirror, then wilted, bracing her hands on her knees and gasping for breath.

Seth immediately held the mirror up to the sun so that the bright rays flashed off the smooth surface of the glass.

Breathing heavily, Elizabeth pushed herself upright and tried to determine the source of the sound.

"Over there," Seth shouted, pointing up.

Tipping her head, she finally located a tiny black dot. Of their own volition, her feet took two steps as she tried to determine the direction of the aircraft.

"Do you think they can see it?" she asked tensely.

"I don't know. They're still pretty far away."

She gnawed at her lower lip, her eyes squinting against the brilliant sky, her gaze fastening on the dot in the distance that grew larger and larger with each moment that passed. Her heart crept up her throat, resuming a new position at the base of her skull, beating a furious tattoo. Her muscles jumped with excitement until she nearly bounced in place.

Swallowing heavily, she fought to keep herself from racing across the snow in an effort to meet the plane halfway. Glancing back over her shoulder, she watched the emotions chasing across Seth's features—concentration, fear, hope, exhilaration—as he flashed the mirror in the sunlight, trying to gauge the best angle to attract attention.

Darting another look into the heavens, she gasped when the plane seemed to turn away from them slightly, heading toward another large range of mountains.

"Damn it!"

She jumped when Seth swore violently behind her. "We're over here," he rasped. With renewed desperation, his hand shook the mirror in a violent rhythm.

The energy drained from her body and her eyes squeezed closed. They were leaving them again. The plane had been so close, and once more they were about to be abandoned to the elements. She continued to watch, her eyes welling with unshed tears, until the tiny outline of the plane seemed to waver. She quickly wiped away the wetness, her shoulders sagging.

Then Seth's lips split in a wide grin and the air was rent with a triumphant war whoop.

"They saw us, Liz. They saw us."

His free hand snaked around her waist, pulling her hard against his chest. Together, they watched the vague shape crystallize and become clearer and larger as the distance between them lessened.

A roaring blast of engine noise brushed past them as the plane dove close to the ground, then swept up and around, maneuvering to face them. Almost immediately, it zoomed past, heading in the direction it had come, giving them a brief glimpse of a colorful company logo and a reassuring waggle of its wings.

Seth swept her into his arms, whirling her around and around.

"We did it! We did it! They've seen us. They'll send help."

She laughed in exhalation. Winding her arms around his neck, she tangled her fingers in the curls tumbling against his collar.

Seth whirled her in a circle until her head spun. When he set her down in the snow again, she had to cling to him in order to keep her balance.

"How long do you think it will take?"

"There's no way of telling—an hour, maybe more. It all depends on how far the search-and-rescue teams have to come."

"But they will be here."

"Yes. They'll be here. Soon."

She grinned, pushing away from him to run to the plane. "I'm just going to tell Walsh."

Her limbs were still weak from the exertion, but her happiness filled her with the energy she needed to climb back into the plane. Rushing to the rear of the aircraft, she called, "Peter? Peter! A plane. A plane has found us. We'll be rescued soon. Do you hear?"

But the moment she peered over the seat backs, she stopped, a low, keening cry tearing from her throat. Blood spattered the sides of the fuselage and coated the seat backs. And Walsh...

He lay twisted in a pool of his own blood, his arm draped over the edge, drops of scarlet dripping from his finger to dot the carpeting below. His throat had been slit.

On the floor beneath him lay Elizabeth's empty carryon bag.

Frankie Webb had taken the rest of their supplies.

Chapter Fourteen

"We're leaving," Seth said determinedly.

He tossed a canvas duffel bag in Elizabeth's direction. "Pack light. Take a change of clothing and all the socks you can find. You'll need a container for water, the rest of the food and the flares."

Panic seized her, holding her captive. "What?"

"We're leaving."

"B-but the plane. We can't leave now. Not when we're about to be rescued."

"That was before I realized how insane Frankie Webb could prove to be. If we stay here, he'll never let us out of this place alive. He's made that point perfectly clear. Once he heads back to civilization, there's no way he'll avoid eventual execution. Maybe he's decided to take care of his own destruction. Why else would he have destroyed the signal beacon? It's obvious. Webb was never planning for any of us to be rescued. He's merely playing a game of cat and mouse until time runs out."

Blackness seemed to be encroaching on the fringes

of her sight and she took deep breaths to push it away.

"But if we go, no one will know where to find us. We'll be putting ourselves at the mercy of the elements."

He knelt in front of her, his features growing earnest. "I'd rather take my chances with the elements. I know how to combat snow and cold and severe conditions. I can't say the same thing about Frankie Webb."

"But we don't even know where we're going."

"We'll head away from the area and climb the summit."

"Climb!"

"By going up, we'll break out of the tree line. We can assemble a signal fire and watch this area. If we see any sign of a search-and-rescue team, then we'll light the fire or the flares and arrange for a pickup there."

The plan was sound, but the thought of climbing a mountain seemed more than she could bear. She was cold one minute and hot the next. Her skin felt clammy and feverish, but she didn't tell Seth. She wouldn't. He mustn't know that she was beginning to fold beneath the pressure.

Seth took her hands.

"We don't have a choice, Liz."

Swallowing her fear, she stared at him, trying to draw courage from his presence. But the hands that took her own were cool and dry and a slight sheen of sweat glistened on his upper lip. Suddenly, she realized that she wasn't the only one who had caught a chill. If she were to lay her hand on his forehead, she was sure his skin would prove as feverish as hers.

But just as Seth had said, what choice did they have? Frankie Webb was completely insane. Why else would he be picking off the survivors one by one?

Nodding, she reluctantly took the bag and began filling it with the required items. Then, on Seth's instructions, she layered herself with as much clothing as possible, and donned Seth's leather gloves.

Just before leaving the shelter of the plane, Seth took her face in his hands.

"We'll go slow. If you get tired, let me know. We won't push things too far, but the trek won't be easy."

She nodded.

"We're going to head west, first."

West? Which way was west?

"Because we don't want Frankie to know what we're doing, we'll go through the woods and circle around to the north face."

Elizabeth was near exhaustion and Seth's words made little sense to her numbed brain. Her confusion must have showed plainly, for Seth drew her close.

"Just keep close to me. I'll break the snow and cut a path for you."

"I can do it," Elizabeth said, lifting her chin and calling on her last reserves of strength. "Don't worry about me."

But as her body was racked with trembling, she

wondered if her words would prove to be as weak as her knees.

IT WASN'T UNTIL they reached the precipice where Michael Nealy had lost his life that Liz gave in to the chills racking her body.

"I've got to rest," she gasped, stumbling to a fallen log where she sat with her elbows on her knees, breathing heavily.

She was sick. There was no getting around the fact. For hours, she'd blamed the altitude, the cold, the exposure to the wind. But there was no denying now that she was ill.

Should she tell him? She'd meant to force herself to move on and on, but her head pounded and her body shook. If she couldn't make her way through drifting snow, how would she ever climb the side of the mountain.

Seth knelt next to her.

"Do you have your gun?"

"What?"

"Your gun. Do you have it with you?"

She nodded. "Yes, but—"

"Where is it?"

She dug beneath the layers of clothing to remove the tiny weapon.

"We're near the spot where Nealy fell off the cliff."

Her shivering increased, as much from the memory of what she'd seen as from whatever bug had invaded her system.

"Nealy had a cigarette lighter. Do you remember?"

Briefly, she recalled the evening when they had huddled together in the plane and Nealy had used his lighter to provide them all with a flickering glow of illumination.

"I'm going to retrieve it."

Elizabeth gripped his arms when she realized he meant to leave her.

"No, I—"

He stroked her cheek. "Don't worry. I'll only be gone for a minute, two at the most. The ice has melted away from the edge, and I'll—"

"No, please—"

"Shh." He bent to kiss her lips. "Just wait here for me. Keep your eyes open and your gun ready. I promise to be back before you need me."

Brave. She had to be brave.

Elizabeth forced herself to nod. She would do whatever he wanted. She would be whatever he needed her to be.

Her eyes clung to him as he stood. He dropped the duffel bag with the scant items they'd kept from Frankie—the flares, the mirror, the matches, some clothing, a whistle....

And Willa's books. Elizabeth had insisted they bring Willa's books.

"I'll only be a minute," he promised again, then turned and walked to the edge. After wrapping a rope around the base of the tree, he began backing into the chasm.

Unable to sit and do nothing, Elizabeth jumped to her feet and moved to the spot where he'd disappeared. Ignoring vertigo and the nausea building in her throat, she peered over the edge in time to see Seth slithering the last few feet to the rocky outcrop below.

The body was still lying in its same gruesome position. A light dusting of snow had partially obscured the details of his hair and clothing, and even from this distance, she could see that a frozen rigidity had gripped the remains.

Her stomach flip-flopped and she held a hand to her mouth, breathing deeply.

She would not be ill. She would not be ill.

But when Seth managed to awkwardly turn the body, exposing the face and the openmouthed grimace of the dead man, her stomach heaved.

The lifeless eyes that stared her way were not those of Michael Nealy, but of Frankie Webb.

Seth swore, nearly dropping the body. Stumbling backward, he stood with his hands propped on his knees, his body hunched.

The time it took for Seth to return to her side was agonizing. She kept staring at the body, telling herself over and over again that she was hallucinating.

Frankie Webb. Frankie Webb had been dead all this time. But if that were true…then that meant that Michael Nealy was still alive.

Michael Nealy was the killer….

"Seth?" she asked as he stumbled to a spot next

to her, then sat for a moment, trying to catch his breath. "Seth? What's going on?"

He shook his head. His skin had paled alarmingly.

"I...don't know," he finally gasped. "But we're heading...back to the...plane."

Elizabeth knew she should argue. She knew she should point out that it didn't matter whether Frankie Webb or Michael Nealy was trying to kill them. Either way, they weren't safe.

But as her stomach lurched and her body ached, she knew that neither she nor Seth was in any condition to try climbing a mountain. Moreover, if any answers were to be found, they would have to be found where the riddles began.

With the plane.

THROUGHOUT their plodding return, Elizabeth kept her gaze fastened determinedly on the path in front of her. She couldn't think about Frankie Webb's frozen body or the implications it brought with it. Nor could she even begin to fathom why Michael Nealy would wish to pick off the survivors of the plane crash one by one.

A breath caught in her throat—half sob, half gasp. Nealy had said he'd been on his way to Aruba for a vacation. A vacation...so why...?

Foot by foot, yard by yard, they traversed the distance they'd already progressed. Liz soon became numbed by the distance, the exertion and the cold. If not for Seth leading her irretrievably forward, his will infusing her own, she would have dropped in her tracks.

She was so intent on her whirling thoughts that she didn't see Seth stop. She slammed into his broad back, nearly tumbling them both into the snow.

Seth moved to catch her with his arm, and it was then that she saw what had caused him to halt so suddenly. There, digging frantically through the snow and the wreckage of the plane, was Michael Nealy.

Somehow, he must have sensed their arrival, because Nealy whirled, then dismissed them both and returned to his digging.

"Damn you, Nealy," Seth said, his voice little more than a raw whisper. Then he shouted the words again and lunged toward the man.

By the time Elizabeth was able to react, the two men were grappling in the snow. The sick sounds of fists connecting with bone and muscle reverberated in her ears.

Panicked, she tried to put herself between them. But, Nealy dodged to the side, lifting a metal rod from the snow and swinging it at her.

Elizabeth gasped when a jagged piece of metal sliced through the layers of her clothing and into her shoulder blade. A warmth began to trickle down her back and she grew light-headed, falling to her knees.

She was suddenly so cold, so dizzy. From what seemed like miles and miles away, she watched Seth run toward her. Then she collapsed in his arms and felt the pressure of his palm against the gaping wound in her back.

But to her surprise, Nealy didn't use the opportunity to attack. Instead, he dropped to his knees and resumed his frantic search around the plane.

Belatedly, Elizabeth realized that Nealy was suffering from the same chills and fever that had afflicted most of the survivors. Hazily, she absorbed Nealy's wheezing shout as he discovered a frozen rucksack hidden beneath a pile of debris.

He tugged at the zipper, sobbing when the fastener refused his efforts. Finally, he was able to open the bag enough to remove a crushed box and a tiny glass vial. His hands shook as he removed a plastic-wrapped syringe and ripped it open with his teeth.

When Seth rose, Elizabeth sank in the snow and rolled to her side, trying not to cry out so that Nealy would be alerted to Seth's approach. Biting her lip, she watched as Nealy inserted the slender needle into the vial and fought to control his chills long enough to transfer the clear liquid. He didn't even see Seth coming.

Whipping the pistol from his waistband, Seth kicked Nealy's arm, sending the vial and the syringe flying.

"Drugs?" Seth growled. "You killed all these people for drugs?"

Nealy tried to lunge in the direction of the fallen syringe, but Seth shot at the ground in warning, kicking up snow and ice and causing the man to flinch.

"Not drugs," Nealy shouted, cowering. He began

to sob hysterically. Before Seth could react, he
dodged toward the syringe again, his hands grappling
in the snow until he managed to grab the tiny plastic
hypodermic. But when he discovered that the needle
was broken, he wept hysterically.

"Damn you. Damn you! You've killed us all,
don't you see?" he said, scrubbing at the tears that
rolled down his cheeks.

Seth stared at the man in amazement.

Nealy's despair dissolved into wild peals of laughter as he sank into the drifts.

"We're all going to die. All of us. But we won't
die of the elements. That would be too kind, too merciful."

Seth reached for the man's collar and hauled him
upright. "What the hell are you talking about?"

Nealy waved his fists.

"I was the one who invented it—*I* invented it! But
did anyone give me credit for masterminding the mu-
tation? No. They stole my work. They stole it!"

Seth scowled, shaking Nealy. "Damn it, you're
not making any sense."

Nealy's face was contorted into a mask of grief
and misery.

"I invented a virus. An experimental virus."

Elizabeth summoned all the energy she could muster and rose to her feet, stumbling through the snow
toward the pair.

"I worked at a secret government...research facility," Nealy sobbed. "I was supposed to be working on an antidote for class-four viruses—like AIDS

and Ebola, you know?'' He wrapped his arms around his waist, rocking himself as he wept. ''But when I stumbled across a mutated strain, I was sure my big break had come—they'd write papers about me in all the journals.''

Seth's grip gradually relaxed and Nealy fell to the ground again.

''Unfortunately, my employers weren't as open-minded as I thought they would be. They were horrified by the possibilities inherent in discovering such a potent viral strain.'' He shuddered. ''So when I was approached and offered three million dollars to steal a sample for a competing research facility...I agreed.''

A virus. They'd been infected with some powerful, unknown virus.

''You brought this...*thing* onto my plane?''

Nealy held up a hand in supplication.

''There shouldn't have been a problem, you see? It was properly stored, properly sealed.''

Seth's expression grew thunderous.

''If not for the crash, you never would have known. But then the plane went down and my carry-on flew out along with that FBI agent. I found the broken container next to where he'd been thrown.''

''Caldwell,'' Seth said.

Nealy nodded..

''So you shot him?''

''I was being merciful. This virus is deadly. It can kill within a matter of hours after contact with open sores or wounds. If contracted through the air, death comes slower, maybe a week at the most.'' His laugh was bitter. ''Seizures, internal bleeding, a shutdown of vital organs, dementia. It's only a matter of time.''

''So Kowalski's death...'' Seth prompted.

Nealy shook his head. ''The man fell on the broken shards—*fell* on them.''

''Willa Hawkes?''

''She was elderly, weakened. When she began coughing, I had to take care of her to slow down the contagion. The virus doesn't become airborne until twenty-four hours after finding a living host. I needed time to get away from the plane.''

He sobbed, then coughed spasmodically. ''If only I...hadn't put the antidote in the luggage stowed in the underbelly.''

So that was why Nealy had been so insistent about finding his bags, Liz realized.

''After that first day, I couldn't afford to stay in the area any longer. But I was sure that you would begin digging for the luggage as soon as possible. So I waited and watched.''

''After killing Frankie Webb.''

''The man was an animal. He was destined for execution anyway. I merely saved the taxpayers some time and effort. In the meantime, his death bought me some freedom. I forced him to switch clothes with me and then...'' He grimaced. ''But when the other passengers began showing signs of contagion, I knew I had to do something.''

''So you killed them,'' Liz whispered.

"I prefer the term euthanasia. Trust me, Miss Boothe, I saved them a great deal of agony."

"While you hoped to frighten the rest of us away from the plane long enough to resume your search," Seth said bitterly. "Why not approach us all with the truth?"

Nealy's lips twisted. "I only had one sample of the cure, and I wasn't about to share." He giggled hysterically. "If that bastard Frankie Webb hadn't destroyed the beacon, I might not have been forced to kill anyone. But he ruined any chance of our being rescued in time and I had to take drastic measures to ensure my own survival."

He glanced at the broken needle and tossed the hypodermic in the snow. "But now it's all for nothing...*nothing!*"

Leaping forward, he tore the pistol from Seth's hand.

Swearing, Seth dived to the side, tackling Elizabeth into the soft drifts and covering her body. A shot blasted through the clearing.

Elizabeth sobbed at the answering silence, the resulting stillness.

"Seth?" she whispered, suddenly afraid. Afraid of being alone. Afraid of spending the last few hours of her life without him.

Lips touched her ear. "I'm here," he whispered. Softly, sweetly. "Nealy turned the gun on himself, not on us."

Elizabeth could no longer contain the sobs that bubbled in her throat. Turning into Seth's arms, she cried uncontrollably. So much had happened—reuniting with Seth, the crash, the fight for survival, death and destruction—only to be told that their efforts were in vain. They would both die on this mountaintop.

A drumming began to fill her ears and she wondered if she would be able to hold on to her wits long enough to say what needed to be said.

"Seth?"

"Yes, sweetheart."

"I love you. I'm sorry I didn't give our marriage a chance."

"Shh."

"No, I need to say it. I need to..."

She broke off when the drumming sound grew louder and more insistent. The noise wasn't coming from inside her head.

A helicopter.

Their rescuers had finally come.

SETH WATCHED in agony as Elizabeth faded into unconsciousness. Over and over, he offered her words of encouragement, but he didn't know if she even remembered the plane that had spotted them or the hope of imminent rescue. He kept telling her that help was on the way, but her body became lax, her skin deathly pale.

Finally, just when he began to fear that he would lose her on this forbidding mountain, he heard the distant *whup, whup, whup* of a helicopter.

Summoning what little strength he could muster,

Seth lifted her in his arms and carried her a few precious yards toward the clearing where the craft meant to land. He got little more than halfway there before collapsing and cradling her in the snow.

In a whirlwind of rotorwash and flying snow, the helicopter touched down. Blearily, Seth watched dark shapes emerge. Muttering incoherent words of encouragement, Seth waited for their arrival, then rejected their efforts to help him as well, insisting that they load Liz on the aircraft first. Then, escaping the hands that tried to restrain him, he fought the dizziness invading his body and stumbled back in the direction of the spot where Nealy lay. Frantically, he dug his fingers through the snow until he located the broken syringe and the empty vial. Then, rolling to his back, he allowed the phantom shapes hovering over him to take control.

Just as the darkness closed in, he managed to mutter, ''We're…infected…need…antidote.…''

Then the world disappeared into a sea of black.

Chapter Fifteen

Elizabeth woke to a brilliant whiteness shining against her eyelids. Blinking, she waited for her vision to focus, then lay stunned, absorbing the evidence that lay before her.

Alive. She was alive. There was no way to confuse the sharp antiseptic scent in the air, the scratchiness of sheets, the tubes and monitors at her bedside, or the television bolted to the wall. Somehow, she'd been brought to a hospital.

And she was alive.

Twisting her head on the pillow, she turned away from the oversized door leading into a pale pink and white hall and a smaller aperture that opened to a tiny bathroom. Opposite, she found a large window overlooking a parking lot, the distant shapes of mountains in the background, and sun. Beside the window was a table topped with vases of flowers. And next to that, a chair.

A smile teased the corners of her lips when she noted the disheveled figure slumped against the cushions. His hair was sun-streaked and finger-combed, stubble lined his jaw, and the hospital robe and pajamas were far from flattering. But Elizabeth had never seen a sweeter sight in her life than that of Seth Brody asleep next to her bedside.

The squeak of rubber-soled shoes heralded the arrival of a nurse, and Elizabeth smiled weakly in the woman's direction.

"Good morning," the woman whispered. She was a motherly type with plump, pink cheeks and short brown hair. Her eyes sparkled with open delight. "It's so nice to finally have you with us."

"How long..." Elizabeth stopped and cleared her throat when the question emerged as a croak.

The nurse patted her hand and Liz noted a name tag that read Madge. "You've been out of things for nearly three days now." She checked the intravenous tube, then slid a blood pressure cuff around Elizabeth's arm.

"He's been here for most of that time—against doctor's orders, I might add," Madge continued, obviously well versed in the fine art of chatting and recording vital signs. She grew silent long enough to take her measurements, then loosened the cuff. "The two of you are the closest thing this hospital has ever had to celebrities."

Elizabeth shook her head. "I don't know what you mean."

Madge made a tsking sound and retrieved an electronic thermometer from her voluminous pockets.

"That's right. You've been out of things through the whole hullabaloo, haven't you?"

Elizabeth didn't know how she was supposed to respond to such a statement—especially with a thermometer in her mouth, so she merely waited.

"About the time your plane disappeared, the cable news stations went berserk with the announcement that an experimental virus had been stolen from a research facility in Utah."

In Utah. So where was she now?

"Anyhoo, the story mushroomed when it was discovered that the prime suspect in the theft had purchased a ticket on a plane that went down somewhere in the Rockies during a storm."

Madge made a note on her chart, then positioned a rolling cart over Elizabeth's lap. "I've got some juice for you at the nurse's station. I'll bring it to you right away. Then, I'll order you some real breakfast," she said as a footnote to her ministrations.

Madge paused and sighed. "Where was I? Oh, yes." She flicked a finger in Seth's direction. "A few days ago, there was nothing on television but reports that the wreckage had been located. A news team went with the search-and-rescue team, so they recorded the whole thing."

She shook her head. "Such awful business. So much tragedy. I can tell you the first pictures of the wreckage were shocking...shocking. Personally, I didn't think they'd find anyone alive—and not because of the rogue virus. I couldn't have imagined that anyone could survive such an accident. And when the television cameras focused on a dead man lying in a pool of his own blood..." She shuddered. "Frankly, I don't think they should show such things, even on the news."

Madge took a plastic pitcher, filled it with water and set it on the rolling cart. Then she removed the plastic wrap from a huge sipping mug with the hospital's logo and filled that as well.

"It wasn't until the helicopter landed on that mountaintop that anyone knew whether or not there were any survivors." She plumped Elizabeth's pillows and straightened the covers. "The camera crew filmed everything. I was in the nursing station with the girls, and we all saw this fine, strapping young man trying to run toward the 'copter. All the while he was carrying you in his arms."

Her voice grew breathless with excitement. "I can't tell you how my heart flip-flopped at the sight. Then, when the rescuers strapped you to the backboard, he refused to let them help him. Instead..." she gestured to Seth "...he stumbled away."

Madge hesitated, then lowered her voice and bent closer as if to keep their conversation from reaching Seth's ears. "Personally, I thought that young man was mad to run willy-nilly away from his rescuers. He kept trying to elude the medics and dig in the snow. Even the announcers were sure he was displaying the latter stages of the virus. Later, we all found out he was searching for the vial of antidote and the syringe."

The woman's eyes glittered with potent empathy.

"If it weren't for that man, you'd both be dead now. The rescue team was able to administer the antidote to you while en route, and by describing the vial to the research facility, another batch was life-flighted to the hospital." She sighed in patent delight. "You've got yourself a special young man there."

As if prompted by the conversation surrounding him, Seth's lashes flickered.

"I'll go get your juice for you, dear."

The silence left in Madge's wake was charged with an overwhelming awareness. So much had happened since Elizabeth had last seen Seth.

Elizabeth blinked, remembering how she'd confessed her love to this man just before she'd passed out. It was suddenly important to her that he believe her words had been genuine. She'd meant what she'd said then and loved him even more now.

"Seth, I—"

When he tried to rise, she waved him back into his seat.

"No. Stay where you are. There are some things I need to say to you, and I don't know if I can finish if you interrupt."

She bit her lip, looking down at her hands and nervously pinching the sheets into tiny folds.

"I—I wanted you to know that it was my fault that our marriage didn't work out. I know now that I behaved badly—even childishly. A-and I have no excuses. There were so many things I should have done. I should have been more understanding. I should have been more open to change. Most of all,

I should have been more open with you about my feelings.''

She took a deep breath. ''I know now that I was wrong not to have told you how much…I loved you. I held on to the words and my feelings like a miser. I intimated my affections for you, but I never allowed you to know the depths of my emotions. Worse yet, I never allowed myself to trust what I felt for you.''

Elizabeth bit her lip, afraid to look in his direction. ''I don't know why I acted the way I did. I suppose that after being raised in so many foster homes, I'd begun to resent the way some people offered 'I love you's' with the same casualness that they inquired about the weather. I never really trusted such pro-testations—and I certainly never trusted my own feelings.'' She shrugged. ''Then when I found out you were leaving your job and you insisted we both move West, I took that as a sign that you were tiring of me and that our feelings for each other wouldn't last.''

She swallowed against the tightness gathering in her throat. ''I was wrong. I was so very wrong.''

''You weren't the only one to handle things poorly, Liz,'' Seth said quickly. ''We came together so suddenly, so powerfully. We should have taken the time to explore the relationship. But by then I suppose I was already beginning to entertain thoughts of moving West and I couldn't bear to lose you. I should have thought things out more, but when our marriage coincided with the pressures of a job I hated, and a life-style I found limiting and chafing, I didn't think. I took the position as a stunt pilot without even consulting you—perhaps because I knew you'd balk at the idea.''

The room pulsed with their mutual sorrow, with the might-have-beens and the mistakes of the past.

Seth sat on the edge of her bed.

''I want you to know that I'm fully aware that another crisis has brought us together. I realize that this might not be the best time to pursue this conversation—and that you're tired and weak and hungry. But before I leave you to rest, I just want you to know how I feel. Unequivocally.''

He took her hand, weaving their fingers together. ''I love you, Elizabeth. I loved you before and I love you now. I don't want to live without you. I want a marriage again, a home, a family—no matter what it takes. But I also know that you need time. All I ask is that you consider trying again…maybe agree to have dinner with me, a date or two, whatever you feel comfortable doing. Later, I'll follow you to New York. Whatever it takes.''

As Elizabeth listened to him, whatever doubts she might have had sifted away. If nothing else, their experience on the mountain had taught her that life was infinitely fragile. She would be a fool to waste whatever future awaited her by maintaining her current course. She couldn't afford to be embroiled in a job she hated with an employer who disgusted her. Nor could she afford to ignore the chance being offered her—to live with the man she loved, to forge a new life for them both. Here. Where he'd already built a life for himself.

Wrapping her arms around Seth's neck, Liz held him close. At that moment, she realized she had no qualms about rushing headlong into a relationship. Seth had shown her in a dozen ways how much he loved her—even to the point of sacrificing his own life for her.

Lifting her head, she took his face in her hands and kissed him, softly, sweetly, then with all the passion that flowed through her veins. Only when they were both gasping for air did she release him long enough to say, "Dinner is fine. A date would be nice. But I'd rather marry you. For keeps."

This time, it was Seth who smiled, his blue eyes warming her from within.

"I'm going to hold you to your word."

She pulled him down for another kiss. "I hope you do. I hope…you do."

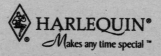

HE COULDN'T FORGET.
SHE COULDN'T REMEMBER.

SHARON
SALA

remember
me

Clay LeGrand's life is shattered the day his wife, Frankie, disappears without a trace. It seems as though his questions will never be answered...until the day he comes home to find Frankie, safe, in his bed.

But Frankie remembers nothing of the two years she was away. Not where she was, or how she got the strange tattoo on her neck, the needle marks on her arms. She has no answers...but someone does, and he's willing to stop at nothing to keep Frankie's secrets—and her life—for himself.

Sharon Sala has a "rare ability to bring powerful and emotionally wrenching stories to life."
—*Romantic Times*

On sale mid-November 1999
wherever paperbacks are sold.

It's
NOW OR NEVER

For three women who find themselves in danger...because of the men they love.

Award-winning author

ANNE STUART

brings you three heart-stopping stories about intrigue, danger and the mysteries of falling in love.

Now or Never by Anne Stuart,
coming to a bookstore near you
in November 1999.

Available wherever Harlequin and Silhouette books are sold.

HARLEQUIN®
Makes any time special ™

Visit us at www.romance.net

PSBR31199

From *New York Times* bestselling author

TESS GERRITSEN

The quiet scandal surrounding her parents' death years ago has haunted Beryl Tavistock. Now she's asking dangerous questions, and the answers are proving that old secrets die hard.

Her search for the truth pulls her into a world of international espionage, and Beryl quickly discovers that she needs help. Richard Wolf, ex-CIA and a man she's just met, is her only hope.

But in a world where trust is a double-edged sword, friends become enemies and enemies become killers....

Gerritsen delivers "thrillers from beginning to end...she can rev up the action in a hurry."
—*Portland Press Herald*

On sale mid-November 1999 wherever paperbacks are sold.

IN THEIR FOOTSTEPS

MIRA

MTG532

*Get ready for heart-pounding romance
and white-knuckle suspense!*

HARLEQUIN®

I N T R I G U E®

raises the stakes in a new miniseries

★ THE McCORD ★
FAMILY
★ COUNTDOWN ★

*The McCord family of Texas is in a
desperate race against time!*

With a killer on the loose and the clock ticking toward
midnight, a daughter will indulge in her passion for her
bodyguard; a son will come to terms with his past and help a
woman with amnesia find hers; an outsider will do anything to
save his unborn child and the woman he loves.

With time as the enemy, only love can save them!

#533 STOLEN MOMENTS
B.J. Daniels
October 1999

#537 MEMORIES AT MIDNIGHT
Joanna Wayne
November 1999

#541 EACH PRECIOUS HOUR
Gayle Wilson
December 1999

Available at your favorite retail outlet.

HARLEQUIN®
Makes any time special ™

HEART OF THE WEST

Every Man Has His Price!

Lost Springs Ranch was famous for turning young mavericks into good men. So word that the ranch was in financial trouble sent a herd of loyal bachelors stampeding back to Wyoming to put themselves on the auction block!

HARLEQUIN®
Makes any time special ™

Visit us at www.romance.net

PHHOWGEN